IDENTITY AND COMMUNITY

The Spirit of the Trees: Volumes I & II

Shane L. Coffey

EARLVILLE FREE LIBRARY
P.O. Box 120
Earlville, NY 13332

BURN THE MAP
PUBLISHING

Identity Copyright © 2013
Community Copyright © 2015
www.burnthemap.com

To the Jefferson City Writers' Group, for all your constructive feedback and support

Contents

Volume I: Identity 1

Volume II: Community

   Chapter One 26

   Chapter Two 33

   Chapter Three 43

   Chapter Four 54

   Chapter Five 65

   Chapter Six 75

   Chapter Seven 86

   Chapter Eight 93

   Chapter Nine 103

   Chapter Ten 114

   Chapter Eleven 124

   Chapter Twelve 134

   Chapter Thirteen 146

   Epilogue 151

Volume I: Identity

Joseph liked the woods in fall. He enjoyed the crisp air, the turning leaves, the earthy smells that rose from the rain-dampened turf. He loved the sounds, though this morning the birds were strangely silent. He also liked the hunt, or at least he liked *his* way to hunt. He didn't understand the noblemen's ways, all charging horses and baying dogs. It seemed an affront to the natural order of the place; they never took so much as a solitary fox but through numbers and brute force. Joseph's way was better, just his wits and stealth against the instincts and speed of his prey.

In the distance he heard a rustle of leaves, a snapping twig. Turning toward the sound, he peered through the brush but could see no shape. With careful steps he eased forward, observing every inch of ground before setting down his foot. His progress was slow, but a night owl on the wing would have made more noise. At last, halting between steps, he heard breathing ahead and immediately knew something was wrong, for the breathing sounded like no beast of the wood, and he felt by hunter's instinct the uncanny sensation of being watched not by some*thing*, but some*one*.

Uncharacteristically, he hesitated, vacillating between calling out and nocking an arrow. Then, all at once, a form burst from the brush.

"Thank the spirits," the breathing voice gasped, "It's you!"

Dumbfounded, Joseph glanced expectantly over his shoulder, but no one was there. Still, to the best of his knowledge, he had not been "you" to anybody in the six years since he'd lost his beloved Delia.

"Young lass," he began, taking a step back then stopping both speech and motion. At first, he had misread the short stature, the waifish clothing, but now he regarded the chiseled, angelic features, the up-swept ears, the almond eyes that looked both intimate and remote. "Who are you, elf? How do you come to be here?"

"They hunt me, Azrith. Please, take me away from here."

"Azrith? Why do you call me this name, never minding I don't know you by any name at all?"

"I know, and I am sorry, but it is a long..." The sound of baying hounds in the distance cut her off. "Please!"

Joseph paused, looking down at the elf through narrowed eyes. After a moment, he turned and motioned for her to follow. He still had no notion what was happening, but he did know her fear was real enough; he could all but smell it on her.

As they fled, Joseph noted her movements through the wood, saw she moved as elves were known to do, leaving virtually no trace despite her speed. If she was being followed, it was only by virtue of the baying hounds he'd heard. He halted, pulling off his outer cloak and holding it out to her. "Take off your clothes," he said sharply, "and put that on." Her shocked expression was the last thing he saw before looking away, but he felt her take the cloak, heard her obey.

"I've got to throw them off your scent," he said, starting to move again as he pulled out a knife and began cutting the elf's travel-stained shift into strips. "In a few moments we'll reach a stream. We have to separate there."

"But I..."

"If you want to escape, you'll do exactly as I say."

Identity & Community 3

"Of course. I'm sorry, Azrith," she replied as they both splashed into the stream.

Joseph shook his head but didn't argue. "Go that way," he ordered, pointing left, to the south. "Stay in the middle of the stream, and go quietly. In a mile or so you'll come to an old, lightning-split alder that's dropped across the water. On the near side you'll find a deep cutting in the bank just above the waterline; hide in there and wait for me. If I don't come back..."

"But you will."

"...then keep following the stream. In a day you'll come to a village where someone can help you."

He didn't wait for her to protest or answer; he headed north, wrapping the strips of cloth around his boots, the better to leave some scent for the dogs.

He had gone maybe half a mile when he heard the pursuit break into the stream. If the elf followed his instructions precisely, the unknown hunters should follow his trail instead. He cursed himself, suddenly realizing the rashness of his actions; still there was no way now to turn back without even greater risk, and so he pressed on, increasing his speed, allowing some distance to open up between him and the pursuers.

After another half-mile, he turned right and leaped out of the stream on the same side he'd entered it, heading toward his most recent campsite. He hoped it would appear to the hunters that their quarry was trying to double back and confuse her trail. The dogs might pick up his real scent once they reached the camp, but he was all through these woods every day, half the time dragging bleeding game or offal. If they could pick up his freshest trail amidst all that, then they would eventually find him wherever he fled, so he pinned his hopes on the belief that they couldn't.

With practiced movements he scaled a large poplar and shoved the elf's clothing scraps into a high fork that was invisible from the ground. When the dogs took to baying at an obviously deserted tree, with any luck it would force their masters to assume they'd lost the trail. With a couple of deft leaps Joseph was back on the ground, retracing his steps to the stream as closely as he could without running into the hunters. He trusted his stealth, however, and ventured close enough to catch a glimpse of them through the underbrush as they passed, three large men on black horses with two more on foot looking for sign and holding the dogs. The riders were not heavily armored, but they sat their saddles as though accustomed to being so, and their faces were cold and stern. He considered climbing a tree and felling them all with arrows, but he had no quarrel with them, no notion of why the elf girl had felt compelled to run in the first place, no just cause to do these men harm.

Trusting his speed as much as his stealth, he observed them for a time, but they spoke little and gave away nothing that helped him to understand the strange goings-on in his woods. Finally, once confident they would not immediately pick up his trail from the campsite, he sped back to the stream and the elven woman waiting in the bank dug-out. She was clearly overjoyed at his return, but he motioned for silence and she remained so.

"Now," Joseph said quietly, keeping one ear open to the forest sounds outside the recess, "just what is going on here? Who are you?"

"I am Kaillë Windsong, daughter of the chieftain of the Windrider clan."

"How do you come to be here, and in such a state as I found you?"

"My village was attacked. Many died, and many fled. I have been running for nearly two days. I do not know why they still follow me."

"Why do you call me Azrith?"

Now the elf was clearly puzzled. "I don't understand."

Identity & Community

"I don't know you; by your introduction I take it you didn't expect me to, but you seem to believe you know me, and you call me this name I have never heard. I would have that explained before things get even more out of hand."

"It is the most ancient legend of the Windrider clan. In the hour of greatest need, when wicked men attack, the survivors will find Azrith, a man of the wood who will bring deliverance."

"I am sorry, Kaillë, but I am not this man."

"But you must..."

"My name is Joseph, and I'm a simple hunter. I don't plan on 'delivering' anybody today."

"But there was more, and everything rings true...apart from the name. Isn't it possible...?"

"It isn't."

"But..."

"I will hear no more of this! You say you do not know why these men are after you?"

"No."

"Well, it's plain enough you aren't carrying anything, so it must be something about who you are. A chieftain's daughter could fetch quite a ransom."

"No," Kaillë disagreed, "there would be no one to pay it. Father and the rest of my family did not survive." Her voice was even and calm, betraying no pain or anger.

Damn her elven stoicism, Joseph silently cursed. *Scream, weep, do* something. "Alright," he continued aloud, "not for ransom...then what? What could they possibly gain by your death or capture?"

"I'm sorry, Az...Joseph... I truly do not know."

"Well, I'll..." Suddenly Joseph stopped speaking, tilting his head toward the mouth of the dug-out. "The birds are alarmed. Your enemies must be searching upstream. If they pick up a scent again, we're done for. We have to run."

Kaillë stood, and Joseph was glad to see she had already

gathered and tied his oversized cloak so she could move quickly. He motioned for her to follow, leaping over the fallen alder and dropping on the far side. Once there, he turned, reaching up to help the much shorter elf down from the crest of the fallen trunk. Just as their hands clasped, a raucous horn blast smote the woods, followed by the frenzied barking of two dogs. Kaillë had been spotted.

Joseph's mind raced. He never doubted his skills in the woods, but they had not been pitted against human minds since the wars. Despite the strangeness of his situation, he felt a pang of guilt for failing to note the enemy's approach before it was too late, but there was no time now for apologies. Instead, he clenched Kaillë's delicate hands and dragged her down from the tree, pulling her into his arms as he darted into the woods, sensing the limp weariness in her frame as he carried her.

He had to move, had to get them into thick enough brush that the men were forced to abandon their horses, at the very least, for he could never hope to outdistance mounted hunters. Still, he realized even that tactic would not be enough, not now. As he moved from the stream, he knew the dark-clad men had seen him, however briefly. Now that they had reason to follow this other scent they had no doubt picked up in his camp, now that they were this close to a fresh trail, there would be no evading those dogs.

One problem at a time, Joseph chided himself. He knew of a place half a mile into the woods where perhaps he could force the riders to foot, draw them into a marshy part of a feeder stream course, gain the high ground... He just wasn't sure he could get there with a spent elf maid in tow.

He barely had the time to try. Charging uphill, he passed a deer run that paralleled the stream and was horrified to realize by the approaching cadence of hooves that the hunters had found it, thundering toward his path just yards behind. Digging his feet into the earth, he tried for a desperate burst of speed into the brush, but with the sudden hiss of a whip the breath seized in his throat, his feet flying out from under him as Kaillë tumbled from his arms.

The world spun around him. He tried to yell for the elf to run, but all he could manage was a hoarse rasp. With perfect clarity, as if in some dream-realm where sight runs faster than time, he saw the girl get her feet under her and start forward into the woods, but then another horse thundered by, its hooves echoing like war drums in his pain-wracked senses. In another moment Kaillë was dragged up off the ground by her tangled, golden hair and thrown roughly across the attacker's saddle horn, all the while screaming "Azrith! Azrith!"

The third horse approached, and this additional layer of percussion for a moment drowned every other sound, but not before Joseph heard Kaillë, her eyes pinned unfailingly to his as she was sped away, scream, "My people, Azrith! You have to find my people! You can save them!" With that, she was gone, her unchecked faith, as absolute as it was misplaced, piercing his heart. A moment later, the last horseman loomed over him, regarding him for a moment. "Just a yeoman hunter," he concluded, obviously unimpressed. "Kill him." This order he directed casually to someone coming from farther behind, then he was off again. The scents of unwashed sweat and dog washed over Joseph as the two footmen approached, one of them leaning into his still-tunneled vision.

"Sorry, coz," sneered a gap-toothed grin as the brigand leaned close, a knife poised to slit his throat. His breath finally returning, and spurred into action, Joseph fought through the fog, reaching up to grab the knife-hand while aiming a savage kick at his enemy's crotch.

The kick landed, dropping Joseph's foe to his knees as the hunter wrenched the knife free. He knew a second enemy was approaching, heard the leaves rustle, turned and threw the knife, more hopeful of slowing the second attacker than of delivering a crippling wound.

The other man reeled back as the knife embedded in a tree uncomfortably close to his face. Still, he grinned wickedly, then called out, "Stitch. Yowler. Kill!" Off the leash and snarling, the two dogs bolted from behind the second footman and charged at Joseph with bared teeth.

Shoving the first attacker, still wheezing, from his knees to his side for good measure, Joseph dropped to a crouch and held his ground against the charging dogs. All he needed to know about these two he had learned earlier in his few minutes of observation from the brush. Hungry and mistreated they were, but poorly trained. Even their tracking was more instinct and breeding than anything else, and what little instruction they had was in finding prey, not killing it. Making a gentle, clucking sound as he held out his left hand, he reached back into a belt pouch with his right and pulled out a few strips of stiff jerky, which he quickly held forward. If he'd ever seen the fight go out of an animal more quickly, he couldn't remember when.

As the enemy stared dumbfounded at his sudden change of fortune, Joseph seized the moment to get back to his feet and draw his own weapon, a long-bladed hunting knife. His skill with it did not rival his mastery of the bow slung on his back, but the quarters were too close for that, and even against his knife the brigands were likely to get more than they'd bargained for. Only a few seconds had passed, and the enemy he'd kicked was still closer than the one who had called the dogs, so he took a risk, grabbed the groaning bandit by the hair, and jerked him upright, laying his blade across the smaller man's throat. "Back down," he threatened, "or your friend dies."

"Who said he was my friend?" the second man asked, keeping reasonably calm, all things considered.

Joseph shrugged. "If that's your call..." He pressed the knife into his hostage's flesh.

The threatened man boiled over with emotion, gasping against the knife blade in anger and terror. Finally he managed to articulate, "Jamen, you bastard. Drop it!"

Jamen hesitated, and Joseph was tempted to make his cut, but he was loathe to kill a man if it could be avoided. "I could probably take you both in a *fair* fight," Joseph growled, "and you can see I don't suffer the need to fight fair. One way or another, I'm leaving here alive. Whether you do the same, that part's up to you."

Jamen addressed his compatriot. "He's just a wild hunter, Derek. He can't be trusted. If I drop my blade, he'll kill us both."

"Please," Derek started begging. "Please, coz, please don't kill me."

Joseph knew he could never slaughter a begging man, as much as he might like to, and the standoff was wasting precious time. His mouth near Derek's ear, he whispered, "Remember what that kick felt like. If you don't stay out of this, you'll *wish* I'd slit your throat." With that, he shoved Derek toward Jamen and dropped into a fighting stance, knife-blade forward. "Come on," he growled to the obstinate brute. "Let's get this over with."

Derek slunk obediently off to the side, while Jamen, looking betrayed, charged in, launching a flurry of strikes at Joseph's eyes. It was an effective attack against the uninitiated, but Joseph was at least a step better, ducking under while thrusting his point up into the meat behind Jamen's elbow, then driving his shoulder hard into Jamen's sternum, sending him staggering back.

Jamen kept his feet, impressively enough, but had let his guard drop to clutch at his bleeding arm wound. A look to Joseph's steadily-held and blooded blade convinced him, and he dropped his knife without further resistance.

"Now," Joseph said, "will one of you tell me what in the *hell* is going on?"

"I'm bleedin' to death!" Jamen cried.

Joseph sighed. For a flash he remembered the crisp autumn morning, the sun-dappled forest floor, the occasional rustle of a soft breeze. How had such a perfect morning turned into such a miserable day? "You," he grunted, pointing his knife at Derek. "Bandage his arm." He reached into his pouch and tossed some dressing material at Jamen's feet.

While Derek worked, Jamen started talking. "We weren't in the battle. We don't get called into the real fights with the soldiers. But afterward, the bosses started getting real antsy. Paranoid, even. They ordered every survivor had to be tracked down."

"Why?" Joseph demanded.

"You think they tell us?"

"I heard something," Derek said quietly, tying the bandage then straightening up. "Master Aglar, he's in charge of the hired army that does most of the fighting, he was giving his report to the Baron..."

"Slow down," Joseph ordered. "Master Aglar and the Baron; these are some of the 'bosses' Jamen mentioned?"

Derek nodded.

"And just who are they?"

"Baron Turov. He was on the wrong side of some war on the east side of the mountains; got his vassals killed and his lands pieced out to the winners. He was exiled. No land, no men but his house guard, and a hefty purse they let him keep. He took up in the old fort up in the pass and put out the call for hired fighters. Master Aglar answered. He was leading a mercenary army, between wars and near to starving. Jamen and me just tagged on in the last couple months."

"Round about the time the Baron started looking for

Identity & Community

weak innocents to butcher?"

Derek didn't seem to have a good answer, and Joseph realized there wasn't one. "Alright," he relented, "keep talking."

Derek cleared his throat before continuing. "Anyways, I heard Aglar tell the Baron that a lot of the prisoners were acting smug, saying how they were going to be freed and the Baron's men all put to the sword by some legendary hero called Alrith or Adrith or..."

Azrith. Damn. "That's good enough. Go on."

"So the Baron ordered that some of the elves be tortured until they told the whole story. I guess some did, 'cause a couple hours later we got sent out to start tracking."

"Any idea why they didn't just kill the girl?"

"Orders," Jamen said. "Elves alone, we kill. If seen with a human or having crossed paths with any, we bring back to the fort to answer questions."

"Think they want to figure out for themselves if this Adrith character is real," Derek added.

"How far is this fort?" Joseph asked.

"Maybe half a day on foot, up into the mountains. But the knights will be halfway to the pass by now; you'll never catch them."

Joseph snorted. *Knights, are they?* He wasn't often on friendly terms with nobility, but he had known several knights during the war. Most were arrogant and naive about the difficulties of unprivileged life, but they were strong and brave and mostly good. While he stayed back with the archers, within spitting distance of the supply wagons and surgeons, the knights risked life and limb in the charge. After he scouted paths and avoided being seen by the enemy, the knights engaged them head on. Joseph's respect was never grudging, but it was hard-earned, and the knights he once knew had earned it. If these brigands tearing up his woods, killing innocents and abducting women were knights, then he was a shank of roast boar. As usual, though, he kept his thoughts to himself.

"You just let me worry about catching them," he said. "*You* worry about what I'm going to do with you two half-wits now."

"You gave your word," Jamen cried.

"I told you I'd kill you for sure if you fought, which, by the way, you did. It's no fault of mine you did it so poorly."

"C'mon, coz; just let us go," Derek whined. "You'll never see our faces again, I swear."

"I'm not concerned that I'll see you...but I'm a little concerned that I won't. Even I sleep sometimes." He thought for a moment, then, "Give me your boots."

"What?"

"Do as I say." His grip on the knife tightened.

A few costly moments crawled past, and with that he was on the move again, the boots stuffed into the top of his pack and the dogs running before him. He knew with patience and ingenuity Derek and Jamen could find their way to safety, even barefoot, but they could never keep up with him in that condition, nor track him down without the dogs.

In half an hour of moving uphill, he broke into the pass and was dismayed to see the footpads had been right. The soldiers must have hesitated waiting for the dogs and handlers to catch up, but when they didn't, the riders had apparently redoubled their speed. The pass was sparsely grown, all rock and hard-packed earth, perfect for riding. Joseph could see them, little more than dots going over the saddle of the pass at a distance that would take him an hour to cover, with them gaining even more ground. He could not hope to overtake them before they reached their keep, nor could he hope to get at Kaillë or the other elves once the enemy riders were safely inside.

Finally, facing defeat, he paused to consider his

Identity & Community 13

situation, to think rationally as he had not done since the girl came bursting out of hiding in his forest. He had tried. He had done more than anybody could expect, risking his life for someone he didn't know, and had he been a moment slower against Derek and Jamen, he'd be too dead now to worry about it. This was a special kind of madness, to go chasing over the mountains to rescue someone who struggled to call him by his proper name, someone to whom he owed nothing. More importantly, this fight was none of his concern, and he had sworn after the war never to fight and kill again unless he had a personal stake in it. He'd shed too much blood, some of it his own, fighting somebody else's battles, spent too many summers away from home being someone else's man, summers away from Delia, the woman for whom he would even now sell out a thousand villages of superstitious, deluded elves, if it meant having her back for but a single day.

At last he turned away from the pass and started slowly back toward his camp. Solitude, nature, the hunt, these were Joseph's life and refuge, not prophecies and foolish heroics. Better to return home, stay out of such trouble, try to keep alive memories of happier times, of his beloved...

Delia was small, quiet, and not overly interesting to look upon, but the first time he had seen her moving through the forest, he had been smitten, her unparalleled grace piercing his soul better than a thousand sonnets a more eloquent lass might have sung. He spent an entire day tracking her, studying her movements, trying to think of some clever pretense by which to approach. By that evening, when first they'd spoken, he'd already memorized her face, plain or not: her tan skin, her long, dark braid, her chiseled features, her gently up-swept ears...

Joseph shook his head, hard, to clear it. "She wasn't an elf!" he shouted, arguing with no one. It was true, she wasn't an elf, but her mother was, the mother who had taught Delia all the secrets of the wood that Delia later taught to him, turning an already-skilled hunter at fifteen into a remarkable one by twenty...and, by twenty-three, one the crown and his army could not allow to go unused. Apart from that skill, she always acted more human than otherwise, at least until the end. In the end, as she became sicker and sicker, she reverted to the stoic acceptance so typical of her mother's people, never crying, never cursing, just going about the day as though everything was fine, reminding Joseph of all the tasks he would need to re-learn now that she would not be there to do them.

One day she even asked if he would love again when she was gone, and she asked it the way he might have asked about tomorrow's breakfast. He had screamed at her then, had cursed her for being so placid, and stormed from the cottage. A few minutes later he had returned, terrified at wasting another second together. Even at his outburst, she hadn't been angry; she understood his human emotions all too well. She simply looked at him and said, "I have my answer, then. I fear you will not love, and I think that makes me sad."

Joseph's pace through the wood slowed as he remembered another conversation, years before, when the King's men had come for him.

"Is the cause just?" she had asked.

"It isn't my cause," he'd spat back.

"But is it just?" she asked again, undaunted.

He nodded.

"Then why do you refuse?" she questioned. "You do not fear death."

"I fear nothing. Nothing, at least, for myself. But I fear for you. You need me here, and I need you by my side. Why must you ask me to go where you cannot follow?"

"Because you are a just man, and when the cause is just, what if every just man turned his back for love? I need you,

Identity & Community 15

Joseph...but the world needs you more...for a time. Then you can come back to me."

Finally Joseph's senses snapped back to reality, and he realized suddenly where he had walked. The grove was beautiful in the autumn sunlight, bugs and motes dancing in the shafts of radiance as birdsong and the smells of earth enveloped him, the power of the place holding him captive softer than a kiss but stronger than any chain. Still her words thundered through him. "You are a just man... The world needs you more..."

Joseph slumped to the ground and wept, burying his face in the dry, autumn grass over his beloved's grave. "How do I go on?" he sobbed. "How do I know the right path when everything that was ever right about me is gone and buried? Delia, please, just tell me what to do."

Then somehow, in a flash, he felt the conviction that she already had. Joseph, on his knees, his face in the earth, became very still. As the dogs whimpered and snuffled at his ears, he again remembered that first day he had seen her in the woods. When he'd finally overcome his fears, he had bounded up to her, quick and silent. He frightened her at first, and she cried out in the Elven tongue. He introduced himself and asked what her words meant. "I called you a tree-spirit," she said, "in my mother's tongue. I have never heard of a human who could move like you."

She'd only rarely spoken Elven to him, but a decade of chance phrases and half-conversations rolled through his mind before finally his eyes snapped open.

Azer, the animating spirit, that which gives life and purpose. *Riv*, an individual tree, or, collectively, *rith*.

Spirit of the Trees. Azer-rith.

"She called me Azrith," he gasped. Then, to the blessed earth below him, "You called me Azrith!"

"I did not," sounded a voice off to his left, "but I dared hope I might."

Joseph straightened and looked over, spotting an elf at the edge of the clearing, so well-camouflaged Joseph doubted he could have seen him at all had he not broken cover.

"Who are you talking to," the elf continued, "that you say calls you this name?"

"I was... It's a long story," Joseph finally replied. "Who are you?"

"I am Tal'onë, of the Windrider clan. My people..."

"Yes, I know," Joseph interrupted.

"Then you are the one who was foretold?"

"...I don't know. I never paid much heed to prophecies. But I'll admit to some strange similarities."

"Will you help us?"

Joseph looked pointedly at the earth, then back, levelly, into Tal'onë's eyes. "Is your cause a just one?"

"My people want only peace with our neighbors. Our warriors protect us from wild beasts and lone brigands, but we do not train to fight whole armies. We wouldn't know how. The enemy lives by murder and theft. They struck without provocation or warning. We wish only to rescue our own from lives of bondage, or worse. That is just in my eyes."

"I believe you," Joseph replied.

"Then you will help us?" Tal'onë repeated.

"Prophecy or no, I'm just a man...but I'm told I am a just man. I will help you...but the task will not be easy. I am a cunning hunter, but taking keeps from armored soldiers is not my strength."

"You will not be alone," Tal'onë replied, whistling a quick, three-note tone. Joseph immediately recognized it as belonging to no bird of his wood, but it would fool all but the most observant of listeners. Three elves materialized into the clearing from the trees, then glanced up as a shadow fell over the sun-dappled clearing. Following their

Identity & Community 17

gaze, Joseph instinctively flinched as five huge, winged silhouettes circled ever lower toward the clearing, then finally landed with a powerful downdraft and voluminous rustling of wings. What space remained in the clearing was now all but filled by five giant owls, another elf of the Windrider clan astride each one. The dogs cringed away, and Joseph let out a startled cry, but Tal'onë only smiled. "Did you think we were called the Windrider clan for nothing?" he asked good-naturedly.

The nearest owl shifted uneasily, and its rider chuckled. "Calm yourself, human, you make Moonwing nervous."

I make him *nervous?* Still, Joseph steeled his nerves and stepped closer. There was no beast of land, air or burrow he could not befriend, whether regular size or huge. Cautiously he raised his hand toward a beak that could probably snap it clean off, then gently brushed the feathers at the side of Moonwing's face.

Moonwing responded with a low, satisfied "wh-hoo" and shifted closer, nearly knocking Joseph to the ground.

"I'm sorry I was startled," Joseph said then, "but I've only heard of such creatures in tales, tales that I was never sure were true. I certainly had no idea that any people had tamed them."

"I don't know that we have," Tal'onë responded, "but we get along together. It is small wonder you didn't know. We keep no secrets, but some things we choose not to announce too loudly to outsiders. This is one."

One of the other riders spoke in Elven. Joseph only caught a few words, but it seemed the owl riders, who'd previously been out of earshot, were asking about him. Tal'onë answered, and Joseph understood the sense of his reply to mean he might be the one foretold but had offered his help, regardless. The elven leader then called the riders to dismount.

"Well, Tal'onë," Joseph said, "my name outside of

harbingers and omens is Joseph, and if we're going to free your people with just me, nine elves, five oversized owls, and a brace of dogs...assuming the owls don't eat them...then we're going to need a plan."

More low words in Elven followed from one of Tal'onë's men, too quick for Joseph to catch even a word. Fortunately, Tal'onë translated for his benefit.

"Ten'ari has pointed out that the one foretold was to know the ways of war as well as of woods. I am not inclined to ignore what help is here, in front of me, for the sake of ancient riddles, but if you have such knowledge it would certainly be a boon."

Joseph shrugged. "I've spent no more time in keeps and castles than couldn't be helped, but I know something of the ways of soldiers. Just enough, maybe. To the north and east is a pass into the mountains. The keep is somewhere through it. Do you think a couple of your riders could find it and get a sense of the layout without being spotted?"

Tal'onë nodded. With curt, Elven commands he pointed to Ten'ari and one of the other riders. In a trice both were back in the air and winging away to the northeast.

"It will be tough to do much real planning until they get back," Joseph resumed. "One thing is sure, at the same time we free the captives, we also need to claim or drive off the enemy's horses. We'd have little enough chance of outdistancing them on foot. How many of your people are being held?"

"We are a small clan," Tal'onë replied, "and many fell in the attack. Some others remain free and well-hidden. It is difficult to be certain, but I don't think more than thirty have been taken."

"Still too many to sneak out one at a time," Joseph mused. "We'll have to rush for a gate somehow, and there's no telling how many guards we'll be facing." Joseph sighed. "You don't need a prophecy, Tal'onë. You need a miracle."

~ * ~

The miracle came three hours later when the owl riders returned; their news was good beyond hope. On their initial approach, they'd seen the castle gate disgorging a large column of men, more than a hundred strong. Feeling this development was worth further investigation, Ten'ari had landed his bird and approached the column on foot to eavesdrop as best he could. It seemed Kaillë's brazen defiance upon her capture and presentation to the Baron, combined with Derek and Jamen's disappearance and their presumed failure to kill Joseph, had been the last straw for Master Aglar and his mercenaries. Finally convinced of the Windrider oaths they'd been subjected to for almost three days, they decided a lethal deliverer of legend, even the threat of one, was too great a foe for their meager pay, and left.

Furious and nearing panic, the Baron sent half his remaining force to scour the countryside with orders not to return until they had brought this "Azrith" back, dead or alive. All that would remain were a dozen men-at-arms and half that number of armored warriors. Better still, the elves were not being kept below ground, instead barricaded inside a converted barracks not far from the main gate. Finally, the western approach to the keep was an area of broken land and boulders that would be difficult to cross but provide ample cover for a band as small as Joseph's.

The hunter spoke quickly as he started moving back toward the pass. "The priority is concealment. If the search locates us, we'll never get within a bowshot of the castle. Second priority is speed. We need to strike tonight, while the numbers are still more favorable and we have the cover of darkness. Tell the riders to fly ahead and scout for trouble; we'll join up with them in the rocks west of the keep to fill them in." As they ran through the glow of autumn afternoon, Joseph outlined his plan.

~ * ~

A few hours later, with darkness blanketing the keep, Joseph crouched in the shadow of the northwest tower, waiting for the signal to begin the attack. Overhead, too high overhead to be noticed by anyone who didn't know where to look, an owl circled each of the four corner towers. Everyone was in position, which meant the last rider, still hidden out in the rocks, by now should have loosed Stitch and Yowler, the Baron's dogs, and taken to the air. Just as Joseph was starting to fear a problem already, so early in the plan, the barks of the two dogs rang out into the still night. Within moments, one of the guards patrolling the wall was shouting down into the bailey of the keep, "Two dogs coming back, alone and trailing leashes. Best open up and let them in."

"We'll open up," a guard shouted from the ground, his voice sounding far away as it lofted over the walls to Joseph's ears, "just keep your patrol going and your eyes open up there. Could be some kind of trick."

Joseph smiled wryly in spite of the situation. It was some kind of trick all right. He just wasn't sure what kind. In a few minutes, though, he would know, one way or the other, and so would Kaillë and all her people. So, Joseph thought apprehensively, would the Baron.

No sooner had the guard on the ground stopped speaking than Joseph heard a heavy rattle from the gatehouse as the drawbridge was lowered and the heavy doors were swung inward. That was good. There was a small chance the guards would have called the dogs around to one of the smaller postern doors on the other sides of the keep, but Joseph had guessed they would use the more direct, less disciplined route. He was not disappointed.

As the drawbridge started to lower, a motion visible even from the owls' great height, the rider above Joseph put his bird into a steep dive. Just above the watchtower's flat roof the owl spread his wings, stopping his descent. The rider loosed a single broadhead arrow that sliced home into the lone tower guard's throat. Everything had to happen quickly and silently now; it was imperative the wall top be secured, without alarm, before the drawbridge could be raised again. Wasting no time, the owl landed silently on the tower roof. A few seconds passed as the drawbridge continued to lower, then a rope snaked down to Joseph from over the parapet. Joseph grabbed the rope and began pulling himself up, bracing his feet against the tower for support. In the other towers the riders would help pull the climbers up, but Joseph's weight was too great for the smaller elves, so he would have to make the time up by his own speed and strength. Joseph poured all his fitness and experience into that rapid ascent so that when he reached the top he was glad the tower wasn't much over twenty feet.

The elf helped him over the edge and opened the trapdoor into the tower's interior. As quickly as he could, Joseph hauled the rope up and shoved the coils through the trapdoor after the elf; the sides of the towers facing into the keep had proper windows instead of arrow slits, so the rope would make for a quick exit to the ground. For all his speed, Joseph was not a moment too soon as he took up a position on one side of the tower's south door, across from the elf. No sooner had he gained his post than one of the two sentries patrolling the outer wall stepped through the door into the tower room. Swift and silent, Joseph grabbed the guard from behind, clapping a hand over his mouth and pinning his arms. The elf struck three times with a dagger, and Joseph felt the body in his arms go slack.

Before he could lower the corpse to the ground, a

startled cry went up from the southeast tower. "Help! Intruders! He-" The cry was cut off, but not quickly enough. Shouts were ringing from the courtyard now, layered over the sounds of drawn weapons and steel boots clanking on flagstones. Joseph hazarded a look below and counted eight men, two heavily armored, now clustering around the doors to the converted barracks. Two more armored men guarded the gate. His side held the high ground; that much was good, but neither he nor the elves had arms heavy enough to threaten armored warriors. Worse, only Joseph's tower had a clear view of the entire enemy group, and now that guards were on the alert and looking high for trouble on the walls, the owl riders would be vulnerable to attack from bows the footmen were already drawing.

Joseph bent his bow as quickly as he was able, but only managed to fell one foe and wound a second before the mob took cover between a corner of the barracks and the gatehouse, the four armored men forming a miniature shield-wall in what little gap remained. No men outside spared the attention to close the gate itself, but the rattle of chain issued once more from the gatehouse as the drawbridge started rising ominously upward. The plan was falling apart, and the greatest weakness of their gambit was now painfully clear: The rescuers were spread to the four corners of the fortress and unable to communicate, much less to regroup. Everything had depended on taking the wall without raising the alarm, and that effort had failed.

Joseph scrambled desperately for ideas until a shrill screech split the night as an owl dove toward the stables. The scream was echoed by the piercing cries of a dozen terrified horses breaking out of their stalls, one of the elves having managed to salvage at least that part of the plan while attention was focused at the gate.

"Go!" Joseph yelled to the elf in his tower, pointing at the stables. "Rally the riders. Drive them at the gate." As

Identity & Community 23

the rider whistled for his bird, Joseph could only pray the elf had understood his human speech. Joseph grabbed the rope and threw it out the window, sliding down as fast as he was able. Horses thundered by not a yard away; the men at the gate shouted and waved their arms in a vain effort to ward them off, but the screeches of three giant owls behind them was too fearsome a sound. A footman shot one beast in desperation, but too late, and the fear-maddened animals trampled through the packed formation and out the still-open gate, leaping the modest gap the drawbridge had attained, while Stitch and Yowler cavorted and barked around them as though at play.

Some of the footmen fled behind the horses; the rest were easily picked off by owl-mounted elves while one on foot secured the gatehouse. The two armored warriors closest to the stampede lay battered and still, a third was struck down by an elf with a heavy stone as he tried to rise. Joseph was about to cheer, but his voice froze in his throat, the victorious elf's expression changing from triumph to agonized shock, as two feet of steel erupted in a gout of blood from his chest. Two other elves grabbed the last enemy's gauntleted wrists, and Tal'onë thrust his knife up into the warrior's armpit even as his friend slumped to the ground in death.

Joseph hung his head in shame and frustration as he picked his way through the wreckage of enemy bodies to the fallen elf. As he drew near, two others were arranging their comrade, gentling his repose as best they could. Joseph looked around warily. If there were other guards, it seemed they were staying inside the keep itself, probably protecting the Baron. The fight was over as quickly as it had begun. Sheathing his knife, Tal'onë reached up to place a hand on Joseph's shoulder. "I'm sorry, Joseph," he said.

"*You're* sorry?" Joseph gasped. "Tal'onë, I..."

"No," the elf interrupted. "You're plan was good. If I

had not allowed that sentry to scream, Ten'bael would still..."

"Damn your hero worship," Joseph spat, "and damn your elven calm. They won't bring him back."

"And neither will your human recrimination," Tal'onë said softly. He held Joseph's eyes. "And I don't care about prophecies or names or destinies." He lowered his voice and cast his eyes down almost as if ashamed. "I put on a brave face for the men, but I never really believed. Maybe I still do not. What I do know is that even though this was not your fight, you took the same risks Ten'bael did. I am sorry for his death, but I am grateful you are not in his place... Perhaps one day you will come to be grateful for that as well. I am in your debt, and had we all perished in this attempt, my gratitude to you would not be the less for it."

As Tal'onë finished speaking, two of the owl riders, with help from within, managed to pry open the barracks door, and elves burst out into the moonlight. Foremost among them was Kaillë, still wearing Joseph's cloak, who launched herself into his arms with joyous tears. "I knew you'd come," she cried. "I knew you would."

"How?" Joseph asked, setting her gently down. "Your prophecy?"

"Yes," Kaillë responded, almost sheepishly, "...and also no."

Joseph sighed. "Please, for once, speak plainly, girl."

"I believed that Azrith could not help but rescue us," she said, "but I knew that Joseph would choose to. You are a good man, my friend." Again she embraced him as other survivors pressed around to clasp his hand or clap his shoulder.

"Perhaps I am," he finally replied, "despite my best efforts."

Suddenly the commotion stopped, and Joseph realized

everyone was looking expectantly at Kaillë. She felt the eyes on her and stepped away from Joseph, leaving one hand on his arm.

"Lady," Tal'onë said, "the Windrider clan is yours now. We await your leadership."

To Joseph's bewilderment, the young elf looked up to him as though asking his guidance. Her trust, all their trust, unnerved him, but he realized he should hardly be surprised. At least half of them had been convinced he was their savior before he'd done any saving; he could hardly expect them to start ignoring him now, Kaillë perhaps least of all, with the weight of the clan on her shoulders and her people still scattered to the winds. They still needed him, he realized, whether he liked it or not...and for an instant he wasn't so sure he didn't. After a long moment, Joseph offered, "The Baron's run off or dug in by now, and his search parties could give up and come back any moment; there isn't time to deal with him. If we're going to gather the other survivors, first we have to disappear, and the woods are still some miles distant. If everyone is strong enough, we need to run."

"We are strong," Kaillë replied, gripping his arm. With that she turned, and, as one body, her people ran out the gate into the night.

And Joseph, Spirit of the Trees, ran with them.

Volume II: Community

Chapter One

After Joseph rescued them from the cruel clutches of Baron Turov, the Windrider elves had assured Joseph of their remaining strength. Despite their recent torments, the elves proved yet stronger than their word, running throughout the night and all the next day with only brief pauses for water. Finally Joseph, their reluctant savior, called a halt, and they stopped to make camp after velvety darkness drenched the forest. Joseph had spoken little except to trade news with the giant-owl riders scouting ahead, but even still the human hunter had been surrounded by elves since Tal'onë's first appearance to him the evening before, so he moved away from the camp and climbed a spreading oak for a respite from the clan, to be alone for a time and drink in the forest around him. Joseph sat on the widest bough, his back against the bole of the ancient tree, the roughness of the bark through his cloak more welcome than the softest down mattress. He'd been awake for two days and a night, but this need for peace was even more urgent than his need for sleep. More pressing still, something gnawed at him; a deep unease had grown as they ran, even after they left the high mountain passes surrounding the Baron's keep and returned to his familiar, comforting forest. He sifted his thoughts best alone, but his solitude was to be short-lived.

"Azrith," called a voice that could only be Kaillë's from the foot of the tree, "may I come up?"

Part of him yearned to decline, but he didn't want to hurt the young Windrider chieftain's feelings any more than he wanted to witness the show of overweening respect that was sure to come as she took her leave. "Climb up if you want," he finally replied, "only stop calling me that." He still had no desire for the prophesied savior's title, nor was he ready to hear another woman's voice call him by the first name his half-elven wife had used for him, even though he'd lost her years before…and though it was only yesterday he recalled her use of the Elven word on the day they met.

"I'm sorry," the elf replied as she pulled herself up onto the bough, balancing her slight frame on the narrower section farther from the trunk. "I'll try to stop. We have good news, though. Two more riders came back, and they brought another three of us."

His discomfort with the growing assembly aside, Joseph agreed this was good news. A pair of owl riders had stayed near the main group to scout ahead for danger, but the remaining four had set out sweeping the forest for other refugee Windriders who'd been scattered. These most recent three now made a dozen they'd found throughout the day, bringing Kaillë's band up to some forty elves. The dogs Stitch and Yowler, whom Joseph had rescued from the Baron's hired thugs the day before, had sniffed out Joseph early in the run as well and stuck by him and the clan like sheepdogs with their flock. "Yes," Joseph replied, "good news."

"But?"

"I'm...uneasy."

"About what?" Kaillë asked, her tone sincere with interest.

"The question I've been too distracted by mysterious prophecies and hunted elven waifs to ask, the one I should have asked in the first place: Why did Baron Turov attack your people?"

"Clearly he's an evil man."

"And?" Joseph demanded.

"Evil isn't reason enough for brutality?"

"Even evil people, even *mad* people, don't hire mercenary armies and organize military raids without a reason, even if it's clear only to themselves. Even some sadistic spirit would be reason enough only if the Baron personally accompanied the attack, but he didn't. I've been watching your people on the run and making camp. It's clear enough they miss their home, but they're capable and content enough without it. So I wager they didn't hoard much in the way of wealth or resources or comforts. True?"

"True," Kaillë conceded.

"And he killed or ran off most of your people instead of trying to take them as slaves or hostages, save the few we have here... so what did he gain?"

"How long have you been on your own?"

"What has that to do with anything?" Joseph shot back.

"Please just answer."

"A few years."

"And you were comfortable that way, if not always entirely happy," Kaillë stated.

"...It is as you say."

"And now you are surrounded by people who respect you, who follow you...who need you."

"And?" Joseph asked.

"And you wonder why you feel uneasy?"

"I don't wonder, I just told you why, and the one has nothing to do with the other."

"Perhaps. Or perhaps it is easier to worry about what the Baron did yesterday than what *you* will do tomorrow." Kaillë's voice was gentle but laden with apprehension.

"That's a blunt accusation to put to your 'savior'."

"It was you who asked me to speak to you as Joseph and not as Azrith."

"Fine. I'd just feel better if I could lay hands on Baron Turov and squeeze some information out of him." Joseph punctuated his point with a clenched fist.

"Please, don't go back," Kaillë pleaded. "We do still need you here."

"Now it sounds like you're speaking to Azrith again."

The gloom hid Kaillë's eyes, but Joseph could see by the tilt of her head that she'd looked down. "Either, or."

"It doesn't matter," Joseph sighed. "Savior or hermit, I'm not going anywhere. If the Baron didn't run off, the rest of his men will have returned, and he'll be ready for trouble. I missed my chance at him." Joseph turned from Kaillë and gazed into the primeval dark of the forest.

"I'll leave you to your thoughts," Kaillë answered. She dropped to the ground with the barest rustling of leaves, and Joseph smiled at her stealth.

~ * ~

Joseph was bone weary, but still alert, when the last owl rider returned to camp half an hour later. The rider hailed the sentries, who responded in their Elven tongue. Joseph never spoke it well, but after hearing it all day, he was quickly remembering much of what he'd learned before being made a widower.

"Did you find any more of us?" the sentries asked.

"No," the rider replied, "but some other lost owlets

aren't far off." The rider was laughing as he spoke.

"How?" asked a sentry.

"A band of the Baron's men are about a mile away to the north, lost beyond hope. His former mercenary commander and some scouts are near them, just as lost."

"Not heading this way?"

"Just going in circles." They all laughed.

Joseph smirked in the darkness as he collected his gear from where it hung on higher limbs. *Maybe I haven't missed my chance after all.* He dropped from the tree and headed to the north, his passage as subtle as a breath of wind through the leaves.

~ * ~

Even for Joseph, the going was slow in the dark, but after twenty minutes he had crossed half a mile and was beginning to make out the sounds of unquiet men blundering through the wood. After a few more minutes he could occasionally catch glimpses of an orange glow painting the underside of the leaves overhead and knew someone must have been using torches, though he could not yet see them through the thick tangles of brush. *At least it's been a damp fall*, he thought. *The fools are liable to touch off an inferno this time of year.* Suddenly a shout sounded in the night, followed by rustling crashes, yells, and the peals of steel on steel.

Joseph took to the trees and leapt from limb to limb, trusting the din of battle ahead to cover the sound of his movement. In a few moments he caught sight of the interlopers and confirmed his suspicions: the Baron's band and that of Master Aglar, the mercenary leader, had staggered into each other in the dark and come to blows. Joseph nocked an arrow and waited, determined to ensure the leader of the Baron's men survived to talk. Meanwhile he studied both sides; he was all too familiar with the Baron's footmen and armored warriors, and most of the other group could have stood in for the two footpads he'd fought the day before, if a bit better outfitted and with movements more savvy to the forest. One man stood back and directed those scouts, though, a man who could only be Master Aglar himself. He was as tall as Joseph, with a shaggy head and chin of steel gray. A cuirass of ring mail, battle scarred but well maintained, covered his thick body, and half-sleeves of chain protected his arms. Resting a great sword against his shoulder, he dealt blows sparingly, focusing his attention on calling out warnings and opportunities to his men, offering no quarter. Aglar was as ruthless as any mercenary commander Joseph had known, which was saying much, but the man clearly knew his business.

Aglar's savvy direction and his men's merciless execution were a lethal mix, and within moments the Baron's footmen lay dead, their armored leader desperately moving to put his back to a tree as Aglar's men closed in. These were not the same sort of undisciplined thug Joseph had crossed knives with yesterday. He drew his bow and took aim at the most threatening enemy, cursing himself for not intervening sooner. Before he could loose, though, Master Aglar shouted in a gravelly voice for his men to hold. The five attackers stopped their advance; two more lay on the ground bleeding with wounds that would kill them by morning, wounds suffered at the hands of the man now at bay.

"You fight well," Aglar said. "Who are you?"

"The Baron's master-at-arms," the voice came back, muffled by the man's helm. "Gren is my name."

"I thought as much," Aglar replied, "but I couldn't be sure behind that pot on your head. You've put me in a predicament, Gren, and I don't like predicaments. See, you've killed two of my men, so loyalty demands we gut you. On the other hand, you have the advantage in arms and skill, so even outnumbered it would cost me another man or two, and I hate to waste them...or you. One way or the other, your life is mine, but give me something of value, something to tip the scales, and I'll let you keep that life in your veins to fight for me...instead of spilling it all over the ground. Speak quickly."

Gren did as he was told. "You left the Baron because it was too little reward for all the trouble, once the elves started on about some savior coming to their rescue. What if I told you the Baron was holding out on you, not sharing all the profits of his venture?"

"That would be a good start if you told me the rest. Say on," Aglar replied, his voice edged with skepticism.

"You must have wondered what profit there was in attacking a village of poor elves. I wondered myself, so I kept my ear to the ground and started putting pieces together...and now I know the truth. That elf village conceals the entrance to the Hoard of Dalviir."

Joseph was hard pressed to stifle a gasp at the name and was glad he'd relaxed his bowstring, lest he let fly an arrow in his shock and bring the whole band down on his hiding place. He mastered his reactions, but his mind was flooded by a surge of remembrance.

Chapter Two

Eight years earlier...

A storm raged across the late afternoon sky, lashing Joseph with cold, stinging rain. He pressed his back against the base of a jagged cliff, inching his way toward the cave mouth to his right and the glow of firelight flickering from within. No sound could be heard over the gale, but he knew what might otherwise have reached his ears: the sounds of heavy labor, metal picks on hard stone.

Beyond that, he couldn't know what to expect in the cave. Rumor had it the enemy, King Ludvarch, or one of his nobles at the very least, had enlisted a rogue's gallery of wizards and treasure hunters to locate the grave of the Mad Sorcerer Dalviir, Scourge of the Fourth Dynasty. Joseph had doubted the rumors, and even if they were true, he didn't see what it could harm. Most scholars agreed Dalviir, if indeed he ever existed, had been no more skilled than any other wizard of his day, certainly not able to create enchantments that could still be active now, some five centuries after his death. Legends grow with time, after all, and what story doesn't benefit from a terrible villain?

Still, something was happening. Joseph's scouts had noted an increase of enemy movement in the area despite the absence of any apparent objective. Joseph's captain was convinced some mischief was afoot, magical or no, and had dispatched the hunter and his band to investigate. Now, as Joseph made his way to the cave, his six scouts would be converging on it from other directions, but unfortunately the sudden squall made it impossible to see or hear them.

At last he crept to the edge of the cave mouth, peering around the corner to see what transpired within. By the light of two iron braziers guttering in the damp wind, he noted seven large brutes smashing the back wall with pickaxes, transplants from one of King Ludvarch's "client states", no doubt. Nearby were three men-at-arms keeping watch and another man in red robes poring over a sheaf of charts and ancient runes spread out on a makeshift table of supply crates.

One of the workers grunted, and a footman craned his neck at a dark patch in the wall where the brute had been working. "Master Viraz," the footman shouted, "we're through."

The red-robed man looked up from his papers with an irritated frown that twisted into a predatory smile when he saw the hole in the wall. He pulled back his hood, revealing a short brush of black hair over olive skin. "Splendid," he crowed. "I'll take over, now that I'm sure where to apply myself." Viraz paced to the hole, his movements so fluid he seemed to float in his robe, put his hand to the wall, and began to chant.

Joseph looked around for the rest of his scouts, knowing robed men and mysterious chanting made a troubling combination, but still saw nothing in the gloom as the wind and rain buried the sounds of anything farther away than a few feet. His bow was strung and ready, but he was badly outnumbered. Ludvarch's colonial conscripts were notoriously unpredictable; some would switch sides in the hopes of gaining their freedom, but others hated foreigners as much as Ludvarch did. Joseph was forced to assume any workers for an assignment like this would be chosen from the more partisan category. If the workers were unpredictable, the wizard was downright inscrutable. A shot from Joseph's bow might slay him as it would any other man, or it might be blocked, redirected, or nullified by any number of sorcerous protections, and if any of them had signs or traces to reveal their presence beforehand, Joseph had no idea what they were. Normally he took his shot and hoped for the best, but without support he could just as easily doom himself and the mission by revealing his presence. In hindsight he shouldn't have been surprised to arrive well before his men; they were accomplished woodsmen, but for all the training he'd given them, none approached his skill. Very few men did.

As Joseph willed his scouts to hurry or his situation to otherwise improve, the wizard, Viraz, finished his brief chant, and the wall around the hole disintegrated into coarse sand just long enough to flow downward onto the floor before hardening back into stone, leaving a portal as wide as a door and perhaps two-thirds as tall. Light from the braziers crept inside, revealing a stone slab in a small, round chamber, all obscured by dancing webs of shadow. Viraz stooped and walked inside, breaking the crust of brittle stone that had flowed over his feet, and Joseph dared a backward look into the gloom. He could see one of his scouts, probably Tobias, judging by his gait, jogging in from the north, opposite the cave mouth, and motioned him to be silent. Once the man was closer, he gestured in their code of simple hand signals, "Where are the others?" Tobias shrugged. Inside, Viraz shouted for help, and one by one the tall, broad workers squeezed into the room, the largest two being forced to their hands and knees to pass the makeshift door, followed in turn by all but one of the footmen, who kept watch in the outer cave.

At last four other scouts arrived, quickly explaining through hand signals and mouthed words that the sudden rains had swollen a stream course at the bottom of the ravine they'd been following. They lost Jerome. Joseph nodded with a frown, frustrated over the deaths of Thatcher and Donald two months before. Jerome's loss would not have happened on their watch. Hesitating no longer, Joseph pointed to Ulf, his toughest fighter, then motioned to the guard inside. Ulf rushed forward with his long knife drawn, silencing the watchman permanently. Joseph had no desire to duck through the low, inner door to be stricken down without a fight, so he arrayed his men in the outer cave, flanking the small door and out of sight. On the far side were Klaus, his second, Ulf and Richard, the newest recruit; Joseph stood across from them with Tobias and Nathan, still his youngest man, though he'd been with Joseph over a year now. They stood with their bows at the ready, waiting for the enemy to emerge into their ambush.

A worker came out first, and the bowmen tensed and waited, bent on delaying until the last possible moment to launch their attack, lest the remainder barricade themselves in the cave until the wizard could concoct a means of victory or escape. A second worker emerged, followed quickly by the wizard himself. In his hand was a glowing sphere, not much smaller than his fist, its light pulsing red. As one, Joseph and his men drew their bows, and the motion caught the wizard's eye. Before they could reach even half-stretch, he swept his fist at the trio across from Joseph, the orb's light blazing through his fingers. Their bows and clothing incinerated instantly, and the three fell to the ground with agonized screams, the reek of burning flesh smoking through the chamber. Joseph's group loosed their arrows. Tobias, to Joseph's right, didn't have a clean

Identity & Community 37

shot at the wizard; his arrow took a workman in the chest. Joseph and Nathan aimed true, but their missiles caught in Viraz's clothing as though it was the densest oak. The wizard stretched forth his hand again. Joseph dove to his left, tackling Nathan into what he hoped was safe cover behind the crates, but Tobias was consumed by a blinding flash of flame.

Joseph protected the young scout with his body and peered over the crates, now blackened and smoking, at the wizard, sure his life had reached its end. His heart longed to see Delia just one more time, and he cried a silent apology that he would not be coming back to her. Viraz strode toward the cave opening, looking into Joseph's eyes. Joseph stared back, unflinching, waiting for the wizard to raise his hand. Viraz only smiled, his gaze as cruel as it was dismissive, and walked out of the cave into the slackening rain, his men trailing behind.

After a minute had passed, Joseph finally breathed again and let his charge sit up. "What are we going to do?" the young man asked, terror in his voice.

"You're going straight back to the captain to explain what has happened here. If all else fails, someone has to know. And me...I'm going after them."

~ * ~

After giving Nathan half his food and water and sending him on his way, Joseph lit a torch in one of the braziers. The thought of his men suddenly slaughtered rose a lump in his throat and clenched his gut into iron, and he looked away from their scorched remains as he ducked into the inner chamber. It was a tomb alright, such as only a powerful wizard could make, a perfectly hemispherical vault formed of solid, black stone with not so much as a tool mark, much less a natural way in or out. In its exact center was a simple sarcophagus of stone. The lid, which had been shoved off so it rested with one edge on the floor and the other leaning against the tomb's side, was carved into a likeness of, presumably, how the interred had appeared in life. Dalviir, if indeed it was him, had been a small man of average features. His lifeless hands rested on his breast, but the taut skin of one held the bones in a rounded grasp, close enough in size to the stone Viraz used to burn Joseph's men. There was nothing else of interest, save for rows of ancient runes carved into the underside of the sarcophagus lid. Joseph had no idea what they said, but he couldn't imagine it was anything good. He considered defacing the letters but had no idea what curse that might unleash. He'd have liked to rebury the whole site, but he hadn't time. Above all else, someone had to keep eyes on the enemy band and determine where they might be headed.

Joseph tracked the enemy throughout the night; even for his keen eyes this was only possible by the light of the waxing gibbous moon that rose shortly after the clouds broke up. Though his enemy left a clear trail, his movements were slow, ever wary for a trap or rearguard his quarry might leave behind, and he dared not make a light to see their path any better. His cautious instinct was driven less by fear than by the certitude that he still lacked any means of engaging Viraz successfully, forcing him to keep his distance and bide his time. All these obstacles conspired to ensure that when dawn came and he stumbled into the first village so cursed as to lie on the wizard's path, Joseph was too late.

It was a hunting and trapping village, the kind with residents who started about their business well before dawn. In the gray light, Joseph saw half a dozen bodies scattered down the main road, and hope stirred within him when he realized they hadn't been incinerated. He sprinted to the nearest body, but his fragile hope was dashed even before

Identity & Community   39

he felt for breath; the man's skin was ashen and cold, his eyes and mouth frozen wide in horror. Closer now, Joseph saw other bodies on side paths and in doorways, as though every resident of the village had been called out of their beds only to have the very life drained out of them. There was no smell, for the corpses were fresh, but the feel of death itself permeated the village, thick and choking.

"Hello!" Joseph shouted, heedless of whether the enemy might still be close enough to hear, desperate to find any survivors and to dispel the funereal silence. "Hello, is anyone alive here?"

"Help me!" a tiny voice called back, distant and echoing.

Joseph followed his ears to the stone rim of a well behind a blacksmith's shed. "Can you hear me?" he called into the darkness. "Are you hurt?"

"Not badly," the voice, stronger now, called back. "I dove into the well when everybody started dropping dead. I guess it worked, and the water isn't deep enough to drown me, only now I can't climb up."

Joseph lowered the bucket rope, and within a few moments the survivor, a stocky lad of teenage years, was back on dry ground. "I'm Dale," he introduced himself, "the blacksmith's apprentice. At least...I was." His eyes strayed to where his master's body lay crumpled in the doorway.

"Dale," Joseph said quickly, "I know what's happened here. I'm on the trail of the man responsible; your people will have justice, but I need you to think, hard, on anything you might have heard or seen, any clue that might tell me where they're going or how to beat them."

They boy nodded. "At first it was just screams and yelling, and then everything went quiet. Then I heard a high voice say, 'Albert, get back here.' A closer voice said, 'I think I saw one jump into the well.' Then the first one said it didn't matter and they needed to hurry. Something about sensing the lines of power still some miles off. Then he said, 'The orb demands much; even this harvest won't feed it for long. I must attune it quickly, not stand about here digging people out of wells.' That's all."

"Lines of power. Do you have any idea what he could have meant?"

"All I could think of was the Old Pillars," Dale replied. "They're some standing stones a couple miles to the northwest. Superstitious folks take their sick up there sometimes, or take cuttings from the grove to put in their gardens."

"Do you know the way?"

"It's easy to find. Just go to the stream at the north end of town and follow it into the hills."

"You've done well, Dale," Joseph said. "A lesser man might have been destroyed by all this, even though his body survived. Do you remember anything else? Take your time; be sure."

Dale nodded as he followed Joseph's instructions, closing his eyes for a few moments in concentration. "Yes," he said as he returned his gaze to Joseph. "Just as they went out of earshot, I heard the one in charge say to save the last of the thorbin root for the ritual. Then something about taking it all at once. I'm not sure. It was getting hard to hear by then."

"That's very interesting," Joseph mused.

"What's thorbin root?"

"Something the enemy uses on their slaves sometimes. It makes them more docile and takes the edge off hunger, thirst, and fatigue so they can work longer. In heavy doses it also brings an unnatural alertness, perfect focus on a task, immunity to pain. They'll fight like berserkers if anyone interrupts their work."

"So he needs their help with that ritual he's doing?" Dale asked.

Identity & Community 41

"Maybe..." Joseph's mind was churning, catching a glimmer of hope and at once shunning it as false, for any hope on that dire morning was hard to accept. Finally he gave Dale directions to his captain's outpost and the passwords that would gain him entry and prove he had Joseph's trust. The hunter then wasted no time in heading upstream toward the Old Pillars Dale had described.

As he ran, his mind continued to tumble around thorbin root, the enemy workers, and their place in the coming ritual. It was possible, certainly, the workers had some supporting task to perform, but somehow that didn't feel right. A thorbin root overdose aided focus, but not precision in the strictest sense, and it was Joseph's admittedly limited understanding that magical rituals had little margin for error...and twice before he had seen the root used in quite another capacity.

Once, he and his men had been chasing an enemy company for days. At last they must have been so exhausted they couldn't even field a proper watch at night, for Joseph had approached the camp to find a ring of enemy sentinels chewing handfuls of thorbin root, all wide awake and alert to the slightest sound. On another occasion King Ludvarch's son had come to the front lines to oversee a battle but found himself badly outmaneuvered. In peril, he'd fed masses of the root to his guard, his servants, anyone within reach. They formed the most savage rearguard Joseph had ever seen, fighting on with wounds that would have twice crippled a regular man. Was it possible Viraz would be in need of that kind of protection during his ritual? Would need it because he couldn't protect himself?

~ * ~

The Old Pillars were shorter than Joseph had pictured

them, only about chest high. They were clearly ancient, though, weathered by the ages but still showing shallow traces of the marks that had been carved on them by whatever race had stood them up in the time before memory. More than this Joseph could not discern from his perch in a silver maple about eighty yards away.

The wizard stood in the exact center of the stone circle; an intricate diagram had been burned into the ground around him, and its lines pulsed dimly with blue light. Just as Joseph had dared hope, the remaining six brutes and two footmen stood in a circle just outside the stones, facing outward and tense with the grip of a thorbin overdose.

Dalviir's orb sat, glowing, on a stone pedestal as Viraz gestured and chanted over it. Suddenly he reached into his robes and pulled a curved dagger. Joseph readied his bow, easing an arrow from his quiver. The wizard slashed his palm, letting blood pool in his cupped hand. Joseph breathed slowly and waited. The wizard seized the stone in his bloody hand and immediately began to scream. The glow in the artifact dimmed, its light seeming to flow into Viraz's very blood and, through it, even into his veins, burning up his arm. Joseph bent his bow to half-stretch, then paused as the sorcerer began to twitch and sway. As the glow spread into his body, bright enough to show traces even through his robes, Viraz pulled the orb close to his chest and dropped heavily to his knees, his head sagging against the pedestal.

Joseph drew back and loosed.

Viraz didn't even scream. He pitched sideways, Joseph's arrow through his temple. The glow winked out completely, then with a thunderous crack the stone shattered like hot glass thrown into cold water. The guards turned as one toward the twang of Joseph's bowstring, but before they could give chase he melted into the forest and was gone.

Chapter Three

Present day...

Joseph shook away his memories as he continued to listen to Gren recount his tale to Master Aglar, who snorted with obvious disbelief at the mention of Dalviir's Hoard.

"You know the war in these parts a few years back?" Gren asked.

"Understatement. What of it?"

"Some folks came over to my side of the mountains toward the end, bringing tales of happenings during the war, tales of Dalviir's tomb and whole villages wiped away with hardly a thought. The Baron was locked in his own struggle for power and sought to verify the rumors. In time he did, even finding record of the remains of Dalviir's resting place. He sent the call far and wide for information of the tomb's contents, but his plans were interrupted. When the coup was launched in Baron Turov's homeland, he mustered for neither side, and the winner called him faithless and sent him here. At last, though, he had it. A treasure hunter finally brought back a rubbing of carvings from inside the tomb, and the Baron spent the next few weeks studying it and working out the translation. He had deciphered the location of the Hoard, and nothing stood between him and it but a worthless band of tribal elves. The rest, you know."

"That's quite a tale, Gren," Aglar said.

"Not the less for being true."

"I don't suppose you have any proof of this?"

"What proof would you have? The Hoard hasn't been looted yet, so there's no treasure, and the Baron destroyed all his notes when he'd memorized the translation; he kept only the original rubbing, and he never lets it out of reach. But of all the stories in the world I might spin to save my skin, why make up one so hard to believe?" Gren's eyes were steady as he stared back at the mercenary commander.

"...Alright. You'll travel with me and a picked force heading back to the elf settlement. If it turns out you're lying, or if you try to switch sides back to Baron Turov's, you'll wish we'd killed you here..."

Joseph had heard enough. He crept back out of the tree and began the long walk back to camp. Less than halfway back he thought he heard a rustle to his left, a sound too large to be one of the night creatures of the wood, and peered after it into the shadows. Nothing was clear in the gloom, and he heard no more.

~ * ~

Once back in the camp, Joseph was relieved to find his presence hadn't been missed. He wasn't completely surprised; Kaillë, as likely as not, had spread the word quietly through the camp that Joseph was to be left to himself. It was strange to think he'd known her only two days, and most of the first she'd spent in captivity, and yet her actions were already predictable to him. On the other

Identity & Community 45

hand, this wasn't his first time facing danger with practical strangers. He knew in such crucibles, bonds tended to grow quickly or not at all. Certainly he had come to admire much about Kaillë, and her people as well, for the matter of that. They were brave, capable, and treated him and one another with a respectful affection that seemed so very rare among humans...rare enough, in fact, that Joseph had spent most of his life avoiding the company of his own kind.

The greater part of him would rather have gone back to his solitude, but he had to admit he was growing to like the elves. When first he'd tried to save Kaillë, he'd even questioned his sanity, but now he knew he would do it all again, and he cared enough to feel a deep pang of shame that he'd almost turned away from the rescue. It was a shame he would not repeat; he would see the Windriders could depend on him until they were out of danger. That was well, for his life, and perhaps many others, were about to depend entirely on some few of them. But for good or ill, that would have to wait. There were still hours of deep darkness left, and he intended to put them to their best use. He picked a spot of empty ground in the camp and, with practiced motions, heaped a pallet of fallen leaves and loam, then sank into the embrace of slumber.

~ * ~

Dawn stole chill and dim into the camp without rousing Joseph, and it was the smell of a cooking fire on the air that first wakened him. The elves only nodded to him in respect as he stirred and left the camp to refresh himself for the day ahead, but those he passed on his way back were more amiable, offering smiles and voicing greetings. After making his way to the hearty smells and warmth of the cook fire, where Kaillë stood directing the assembly of their meager provisions into a reasonably appetizing breakfast, Joseph asked about the behavior. In truth, he was only mildly curious, but even his sorely-wanting social graces suggested news that doomed half the continent was not an appropriate opening to conversation.

"Our people are one," Kaillë replied, "but the whole is diminished if each is not allowed a private life and feelings. Except among intimates, it is thought rude to take undue note of a person's appearance or activities until they've made themselves ready for fellowship with the group. It's easier when people start the day in their dwellings, but we do our best when we're living under the leaves and stars.

"Come on, now, Joseph, enough talk. You must be famished. There wasn't much time, but we've managed a few rabbits and found some herbs to season them. A band should be back any minute with forage; the season is too late for mushrooms, but I'm hoping for some wild grains or tubers. We're preparing what we can now, but we still need to improvise something to hold water so we can stew..."

"Kaillë," Joseph interrupted, "can you work some of that rabbit into thin strips and roast them quick on a rock? We need some travel-ready provisions as soon as can be managed."

Kaillë's light demeanor changed immediately. "Is something wrong, Joseph?"

"I'd like to speak with you and Tal'onë alone, please."

"Of course." Kaillë left preparations for the meal in the care of another elf and motioned for Tal'onë, leader of the Windriders' few remaining warriors, to follow her. In a few moments they were sheltered behind an outcropping and out of earshot from the rest of the camp.

"Tell me what you know of the Hoard of Dalviir," Joseph began.

"What is the Hoard of Dalviir?" Tal'onë responded, puzzled.

Identity & Community 47

"An old human story," Kaillë answered, "a legend about a trove of magical artifacts. Joseph, why did you need to speak to us privately about that?"

"Are you being honest with me?" Joseph asked, his eyes narrowing.

Kaillë's face went slack with hurt. "Az...Joseph, please don't ask that. How could I ever lie to you?"

Joseph sensed her sincerity but pressed on, relating all he had seen and heard the night before, as well as his brief encounter with Dalviir's magic during the wars. "So," he finished, "the Baron's man said the Hoard was located somewhere in your village."

"He's lying," Tal'onë insisted. "The Baron never questioned any of our people about the Hoard."

Kaillë shook her head though. "The Baron may have realized somehow that we were ignorant of the Hoard and chosen to keep his secret. Perhaps there is some mistake...in fact I feel there must be, but the man Joseph heard wasn't lying. He spoke of the carvings in Dalviir's tomb, and that can't be just a coincidence, can it?"

"No," Joseph replied. "Only my captain and I knew of those carvings, and he took the secret to his grave. Nobody else could have known unless they'd been to the tomb."

"The workmen knew," Tal'onë pointed out.

"They *did*," Joseph rebutted. "There's a reason thorbin root is only a last resort; it demands a heavy price when the effects wear off. It's unlikely any of those men lived out the day."

"Then the Master at Arms' story was true, as you say, Joseph," Tal'onë conceded, "but that only proves the Baron believed the Hoard was in the village. It must be as you said, Chieftain Kaillë, there must be some kind of mistake."

"I hope there is," Joseph said, "but the consequences are too dire to leave that to chance. I need to go back to your village and see for myself, but I don't know the way."

"We will all return..." Kaillë began.

"No," Joseph protested sharply. At a harsh look from Tal'onë, he tempered his words before continuing. "I'm sorry, Kaillë; these are your decisions, and you have to lead your people by your own judgment, but if you value my counsel, you won't return to that village. Whether or not the Hoard is really there, the Baron believed it, and the treasure hunter who provided the rubbing might have sold dozens of copies. If anybody else is able to translate the runes, there could be more bloodshed over that place."

Kaillë nodded, her eyes distant, and Joseph could see a dying flicker, demise of the last ember of hope that her people might someday return home.

"Joseph is right," Tal'onë added, "it's too dangerous for you there, my lady, but I will accompany Joseph, and the owl riders as well..."

Joseph scowled at the pattern quickly developing in the conversation before objecting a second time. "I'm sorry, Tal'onë, but that isn't the answer either. The owl riders are too important to take away from your people; they can scout for danger and find more of the Windriders who are lost. I might have considered taking one or two, but after the attack on the keep, the Baron's men will be looking to the skies for trouble, and your owls have no protection against a good enough archer. As for you, Kaillë was raised to lead the clan, but not its warriors. That's your duty; they'll need you here if you run into the armed kind of trouble."

The elven warrior nodded. "Tell us how we can help, then," Kaillë prodded.

"Tal'onë, you have a second-in-command, Tes...?"

"Tes'oriv."

"Yes. I need Tes'oriv to travel with me and lead three or four more of your people, those you can spare that know at least a little of the ways of weapons. I need men of a level

Identity & Community 49

head, people I can trust. I'll be setting out before midday, well before, if possible."

"You shall have them." Tal'onë left to pick Joseph's band, leaving the hunter alone with Kaillë.

"You can trust *me*..." the elf maid hazarded.

"Kaillë," Joseph replied, "after I forbade Tal'onë to go because he's too needed here, did you really think I'd agree to take you along?"

"I didn't think it. But I did hope for it. I don't really want you to go at all. What if the story about the Hoard is true? There could be great danger."

"I know, but I can't stand by when something so evil is at risk of happening. You helped me to remember that, you know. You should be glad I'm going."

"I'm glad you're that kind of man, but I'd rather you could be that kind of man without being so far away. I know I can't talk you out of going, but at least take me with you."

"We both have our duties, Kaillë, and yours are here. Don't worry; I'll see you again when mine are done." He put his hand on her shoulder, doing his best to reassure her, and she leaned her cheek for a moment against his hand. Then he headed back toward the camp to prepare for the journey, leaving Kaillë to her thoughts, just as she had done with him the night before. She didn't call after him or offer further argument, only standing silent, but for all her elven stoicism, Joseph, as he left, wiped absently at a single spot of moisture on the back of his hand. Then a sudden movement caught his eye up above and to his left, but it seemed no more than a bird starting away at his passage.

~ * ~

When Joseph returned to the camp, Tal'onë and Tes'oriv had already chosen scouts for Joseph's mission.

"Joseph," Tal'onë began, "by now you know these

men's faces, but we haven't had time for introductions. These are Tes'oriv, my second, and Ten'daren, Ten'sael and Ten'vahlë. They are young, but wise in the crafts of the wood and skilled with knife and bow. They are eager to serve you."

"My thanks," Joseph replied. "Have the foragers returned? We'll need supplies."

"We'll have all we need," Tes'oriv replied, his elven accent thick. "Everything from this morning is being prepared for travel."

"You've got a lot of hungry people here," Joseph objected.

"None too hungry to find their own food, and we have the time," Tal'onë answered. "Thanks to your tale, we know that nobody is looking for us anymore. We can remain here and regain our strength."

Joseph was tempted to protest further, but he needed the time the elves were saving him, and he was grateful for it. "Alright," he said. "Gather your things and pack the supplies. We'll leave in a quarter hour." He looked over his shoulder at the thick, rumbling clouds that shrouded the mountains. "I hope it'll be quick enough."

Joseph set about his own preparations: mending a torn seam on his cloak, waxing his bowstring, filling water skins. By Joseph's reckoning, it would be at least two days of travel back to the elf village, longer if they had to stop for forage along the way. He doubted the Baron had much skill in the woods, but the elves had been going the wrong way, giving Turov probably half a day's head start. It was a lot of time to make up.

Finally Joseph lifted his head from his tasks and saw the four elves heading toward him across the camp. "Stitch," he shouted. "Stitch, come!" Momentarily the dog loped up to Joseph, who praised him and rewarded him with a piece of jerky. Once the elves had joined them, Joseph only

Identity & Community

nodded once, then struck out to the north.

~ * ~

The going was easy for several hours; the elves moved swiftly and never flagged. Joseph couldn't help but envy their endurance, a trait he had cultivated through years of struggle and determination that came as naturally to the elven race as breath.

Joseph was just calling the third halt for water when a clamor of squawks and rustling wings exploded from a nearby tree as all the birds shot upward. Joseph caught Tes'oriv's eye and glanced to the tree.

"Ten'sael, go," the elven lieutenant commanded. As the younger elf hurried off, Joseph was impressed by Tes'oriv's sharp perception. Throughout their run the day before, Joseph had noticed his initiative and ability to infer an order from Tal'onë based solely on a look or gesture. Joseph was thankful to have such skills at his disposal, especially if danger did threaten. Thunder rumbled once more from the mountains, and Joseph eyed a nearby tree, wondering if he should climb up above the canopy for a better view of the weather. After a brief internal debate he decided against it; whatever his view might reveal, if his enemies pressed on through the storm, he could lose valuable time in delay, and if they didn't it would present a rare opportunity to make up ground. He was resolved to keep moving.

In any case, the storm would spend most of its fury hurling itself against the distant peaks. His chief concern was with a stream that cut across their path a little over two leagues ahead. Normally it was only ankle-deep in autumn; however, the general dampness this year would have it running shin-deep to start with, and a sudden storm over its headwaters in the east could make the situation far different.

After a few moments, Tes'oriv drew up to Joseph's right side and cleared his throat. "Report," Joseph said, recalling his military days.

"Ten'sael found nothing unusual in the area, Azrith," Tes'oriv stated.

Joseph looked down at the shorter scout and cocked an eyebrow. "You're a true believer, then? Or you just think you're *supposed* to call me that?"

"The words of my ancestors guide me. Their wisdom is my truth. How else should it be? They said you would be here, and here you are."

"Your belief is your own, but my name is *my* own, and my *name* is Joseph. Understand?" Joseph said.

"No, but I will obey."

"Good enough, at least for now. Last time I came through these parts, there was a spring near here, but that's been a few years ago, and the brush has changed. Fan out and look for it, please; our water skins are getting light."

Tes'oriv set to the task without hesitation, and Joseph grimaced at the younger elf's blind devotion. Had he not led enough young men to their deaths in the war, that he should be forced again to lead a company?

~ * ~

The elves found the spring in short order, and after drinking their fill and filling their skins, the band was off once more. The woods grew thicker as they progressed, and despite the group's talent for traversing the forest, nearly three hours had passed before they reached the stream Joseph had been silently dreading. When he saw it, his worst fears were realized.

The stream had overflown its banks, shoving limbs and other forest debris down its long slope, much of which was pulled into the fast-moving corridor of deepest water now at the center of the stream course.

    Joseph weighed his options. Aglar may well have made his crossing before the storm surge, and the Baron, setting out from his keep, would have avoided this obstacle altogether. With no similar barriers on the remainder of the path back to the elf village that might slow the enemy, any delay would result in a direct loss of precious time. The headwaters were hours of hard hiking into the mountains and storm, simply waiting for conditions to improve could take even longer, and the closest bridge was over a day away, amid the towns and farmland out on the flats. There was no choice but to cross.

Chapter Four

Joseph looked down at the elves, all below his shoulder. He didn't doubt for a moment their courage or even their strength, despite their size, but here was a situation in which the simple distance between feet and head was paramount. "I'll go across first and sound out the depth," he announced. "I think we have enough rope in the supplies to span the stream. I'll anchor my end on the other side."

As Joseph shrugged off his pack, the elves searched their own for the longest length of rope and knotted it around a leaning hornbeam by the stream. "Who's the strongest swimmer?" Joseph asked as he rolled up his cloak and stowed it in his pack.

"Me," Ten'daren spoke up.

"You'll come across last," Joseph ordered, speaking slowly and with clear gestures to ensure the less fluent elves understood. "Each of you, while waiting for your turn to come across, find fallen boughs or deadwood to lash together and secure the packs on top. Ten'daren, when all the rest are over, untie the rope from the tree, tie it to the raft, and we'll haul it, and you, across. You'll have to help

Identity & Community 55

support the supplies; they're likely to get wet, but at least not completely drenched. Understand?"

The elves nodded.

Joseph took hold of the free end of the rope and stepped into the stream. The water was chill, but he forced himself not to rush. By the center of the span, the water had passed his ribcage, and he found himself fighting for every step, digging his feet into the silt and creek stones to keep from being swept away. Stitch swam past him, intent on the far side but showing only confidence as the stream swept him downstream from Joseph. The dog could parallel the stream course through the heavy brush faster than any of them, though, so by the time Joseph finished his crossing, the hound was already waiting with a wagging tail on the far bank.

Joseph slogged out of the stream and secured his rope to the nearest tree, leaning back to keep the rope taught as he tightened the knot. Tes'oriv came across next, determined not to let his men use the rope until he'd tested it for himself. Joseph could tell his feet were only just staying planted at the deepest point, but he made it across with no trouble, nodding to Joseph as he exited the water. Ten'vahlë came next, the shortest of the four. He was barely a third of the way across when his feet could no longer touch bottom, the fast current shoving him downstream so his body was at an angle as he held onto the rope. The elf focused on the far bank and kicked his feet furiously as he pulled himself forward hand over hand.

A scattering of dead leaves and broken sticks flowed by, reminding Joseph of the debris he'd seen earlier. Casting a glance eastward, he cursed as a split tree trunk rushed from the steeper slopes upstream, a mass of smaller boughs and branches at its top catching the force of the water and driving the log down the center of the stream like a dart.

"Ten'vahlë, hold on!" Joseph shouted. The elf looked

over and saw the danger in time to brace himself, but he had nowhere to go. The trunk thudded into his chest, shoving him to the side and breaking the grip of his left hand. As the current seized his body, the branches of the trunk snagged around him, throwing all the force of the water pushing against the tree into Ten'vahlë's one, cold-numbed hand. He clung for a moment, the watchers on the bank shouting for him to hold on, as narrow branches snagged on the guide rope, but at last the flotsam broke free and shot down the stream, taking Ten'vahlë with it.

Joseph sprinted for the water, fighting through the shallows until he could reach a depth for proper swimming. The grasping branches prevented Ten'vahlë from treading water to any great effect; he only hung on grimly to the floating tree that threatened to spin and dunk him under at any moment. Just as Joseph took his first proper strokes into the stream, Ten'vahlë's hand shot up at an overhanging branch on the far side of the stream. His reach was a handsbreadth short, but suddenly a hand dropped down from the bough and tightened around his wrist. He took hold of his rescuer's wrist in turn and kicked mightily at the water and branches below him, shoving clear of the stream and swinging up into the tree.

Joseph could only hope this apparent savior had no dark motives as he returned to the stream's edge and made his way back to Tes'oriv. A moment later, Ten'vahlë, soaked but otherwise none the worse for his dunking, emerged from the brush with another elf, about his own height, in a deeply hooded cloak. This elf threw the hood back, and the other elves gasped and bowed as Joseph growled, "Oh, *hell*."

Kaillë stood on the far bank with apprehension in her eyes but a defiant tilt to her chin as Joseph glared at her.

"No," Joseph called, "I did not agree to this. You have to go back."

Identity & Community

Tes'oriv touched his elbow. "With respect, Azrith, even if the Chieftain agreed, darkness will come in two or three hours. We dare not send her back alone."

Joseph sighed. "And I dare not leave my band divided overnight or spare the men to escort her back. Well played, Kaillë," he muttered too quietly for Kaillë to hear and too quickly for Tes'oriv to interpret. "Fine," he shouted. "I'll make the crossing again and bear Kaillë across."

Joseph sent Tes'oriv upstream to watch for debris and waded back into the cold stream. With the rope now secured for a handhold, his crossing was smooth, and he quickly reached the other side. Now that he brought his withering stare closer, Kaillë's eyes finally flicked down. Joseph hoisted her up without a word and plunged back into the stream.

"Every time we meet," Kaillë said softly as she clung to him, "you're sending me into a stream," referring to their first encounter only three days before.

"I'm sorry I'm not quite tall enough to keep you from getting partially soaked. That sort of thing happens when you leave the safety of the camp."

"I know you've had to face much about who you are these last few days, but don't forget who I am. I am not one of your human princesses to shelter in some stone tower. I am Kaillë Windsong, Chieftain of the Windrider Clan. I have needed much from you these past days, but I can offer much as well."

"I would have you give your best to your people."

"Tal'onë was my father's closest advisor. He can watch over them for a few days. My place is on this quest...with you."

"And Tal'onë agrees?"

"Tal'onë obeys."

Joseph scowled at the unabashed command in her words, his free spirit affronted, but he had to respect her confidence. She had found strength through her ordeal, setting aside her initial shock and claiming her place with the stoicism typical of her people.

Soon they had reached the other side, and Joseph set Kaillë gently down. "It wasn't my meaning to defy you, Azrith," Kaillë whispered. "I came as my heart led me. If you tell me to go back, I will, but I'm asking you not to."

"Who do you ask?" the hunter pressed.

Kaillë met his eyes. "I ask Joseph."

Joseph held her gaze. "I can't promise to keep you safe. I can't put one life above the others."

"I would never ask that," Kaillë assured.

"And my orders must be final if I am to lead this expedition. You must make that clear to the men."

"I will."

Joseph nodded. "Very well."

~ * ~

The remainder of the crossing went smoothly, though twice they had to pause to wait for debris to pass by, and once Joseph was forced to wade out and clear large limbs that snagged on their rope. At last they hauled Ten'daren across with the packs on their makeshift ferry as he swam against the current to prevent the supplies from being upset or dragged too far downstream.

They pressed on for two more hours until sunset, when the falling temperature started to tell heavily on their still-damp frames. Even then, Joseph urged them on for the better part of the next hour, hoping to find a cave he had sheltered in once before. At last he located it and ushered the band inside. Even Stitch was exhausted, and they had no sooner started a fire and laid their packs out to dry than they started dropping off to sleep. Joseph considered setting a watch, but the band was in sore need of rest, and the cave was difficult to find for anyone who didn't know it was there. Even the glow of their fire would be mostly hidden from the outside by a sheltering outcrop of rock. Since the person following them had turned out to be Kaillë, he reasoned their greatest enemy now was probably fatigue...

~ * ~

The cave lay in deep shadow when Joseph awakened. The fire had burned out, and the westward-facing cave mouth hid the sun, permitting little light and making it impossible for Joseph to be sure how long he had slept. The hunter went outside to relieve himself and check the time and was pleased to see dawn still merely kissed the land. They'd made good progress the day before as well, despite the challenges crossing the stream; there was an hour to spare for a proper breakfast before they had to set out again. Joseph located some dry brush and dead boughs, then went back inside to rekindle the fire. A few embers still held some heat, glowing faintly at his breath. Feeding the heart of the coals with dead leaves, followed in due time with the brush and larger pieces he had foraged, Joseph had a respectable cook-fire crackling by the time the other elves began to stir. In its light, he turned to search the supplies for the best ingredients to begin the meal.

It was only at that moment he realized all their supplies were missing. Seasoned though he was, Joseph could not stifle a call of alarm laced with utmost confusion. The elves questioned his outburst, and he replied, "The food is gone! Not just the food, all the gear, the packs, everything but what we slept in. How is that possible?"

"A thief," Tes'oriv concluded.

"That came in without waking any of us? Even Stitch didn't make a sound during the night. Did anybody hear or see anything?" The elves looked to the floor and made no reply. Kaillë looked hurt. "If I blame anyone, it's myself," Joseph clarified. "We just have to know what happened so we can get the supplies back. We may be going into a fight at the end of this march, which I'd rather not do on an empty stomach, and water will start getting more scarce as we get closer to the higher slopes. A thief seems the only explanation, but then why leave us alive and unbound? He didn't even take our weapons."

As Joseph spoke, Ten'sael pulled a burning brand from the fire and paced to the cave entrance, bending low to the ground. Tes'oriv went with him.

"If they didn't at least tie us," Kaillë reasoned, "they must have been very confident that we couldn't follow."

"Or they wanted us to follow," Tes'oriv called. "Joseph, look. There are tracks on top of ours coming in." Ten'sael spoke rapidly in Elven speech while pointing further down the knoll outside. "And there," Tes'oriv translated, "once out of earshot, the packs were dropped and dragged. No effort to hide the marks, and this was left." Tes'oriv held up a single, black feather. It might have been blown in from the forest but for a pair of silver beads and a short leather thong tied to the shaft, as though it had been used for adornment.

Joseph looked at Stitch as he walked over to the tracks Ten'sael had found. "Skilled enough to get in and out of here at least twice, which it would have taken to carry all our packs, without alerting anyone, but careless enough to drop an ornament even knowing they were leaving a bloodhound at their back? Doesn't seem likely, does it?"

Tes'oriv shook his head. "We're being lured, Joseph."

"Well, if they wanted us dead, at least some of us would be so, and we need those supplies. Stitch!" The dog loped over, and Joseph held the feather out to him. "Here you go, boy. Get the scent." As the dog sniffed, Joseph addressed the rest of the crew. "Tes'oriv, you and Ten'daren stay behind to make sure we haven't missed any other clues. When you're satisfied, douse the fire and follow with all the stealth you can muster. The rest of us will follow the tracks; if there's a trap at the end of them, it's up to you to spring us from it."

~ * ~

The tracks disappeared after a hundred yards, but the thief, it seemed, had done nothing to confuse the trail. Stitch's nose led them in as straight a line as the forest allowed for nearly three-quarters of a mile, where the trail led into a well-cleared path that ran between a narrow brook running a dozen yards to the left and a short embankment on the right. Suddenly a voice rang out from the trees farther ahead, "That's far enough." It was a woman's voice, and the tone was playful, the pitch just a note lower than average.

"Who's there?" Joseph shouted, his right hand straying to his quiver.

"I'm called Rook," the voice answered. "You don't need your bow, hunter. If I wanted any of you dead, you'd be dead."

"Show yourself, then."

A small, lithe shadow dropped down to the path from a low bough, adding an artful flip to the fall and landing in a crouch. The form stood and advanced, the silhouette becoming clearer with each step in the dawn light. The woman was young, perhaps in her twentieth autumn, of a mousey build and barely taller than Kaillë, though she was human. Her sandy hair was cropped short, and on a belt over a tight leather jerkin and leggings she wore a long knife at either hip, but her hands were empty as she approached Joseph. "Here I am," she said, turning a fleet pirouette. "Now what?"

"You're young," Joseph said, "and obviously foolish, so I'm trying to be patient, but don't turn your back again. I won't pass the opportunity the second time."

Rook only gave a sly look and waited for Joseph to continue.

"Where are our supplies?" Joseph demanded.

"Hidden," Rook replied. "Agree to my terms, and I'll lead you straight to them, might not even be out of your way. Otherwise, I'm sure you'll find them eventually, but it will cost you time I know you don't have."

"You know?" Joseph asked. "So it's you who's been spying on me all yesterday."

"The same."

Joseph was tempted to seize the cheeky lass and force the truth out of her, but he wasn't the torturing kind, and the cool confidence in her eyes assured him she would call his bluff if he started making threats. Before he could decide what to do next, Kaillë stepped forward, saying "What are your terms?"

Joseph scowled at her, but Rook answered without delay. "Take me with you. I've heard all you've said, and it sounds to me like this Hoard is pretty valuable loot. Give me first choice of the baubles, and the supplies, and my services, are yours."

"Why would we trust a thief?" Joseph spat.

"She who can steal *from* you can steal *for* you, for the right price," Rook replied, undaunted. "Taking your gear is good for leverage, but even better as my bona fides. You see my skill firsthand. You know I can be useful in whatever you're up against."

"As it stands," Kaillë pointed out, "and as you know if you've been following us, we aren't even sure this Hoard is real. Even if it is, our quest is to deny it to our enemies by any means necessary. These objects are not mere

Identity & Community

baubles; they are artifacts of great power and danger. Why would we let you take one?"

As they spoke, Joseph gestured behind his back to Ten'sael and Ten'vahlë, and the two began creeping out to the sides, seeking to encircle Rook.

"I have no interest in burning towns or melting livers or any of that other rot from the legends. First pick is mine, but nothing dangerous, I swear. Pick your own expert, and I'll even hang around long enough to let him verify my piece is harmless."

"Why so accommodating?" Joseph asked, his eyes narrowing. "I have to admit, you seem to be holding the better cards."

Joseph thought he saw Rook's mouth twitch, but he couldn't be sure.

"Look, I'm just being honest," the thief replied. "But it's like you said, I've got all the cards, so why not just agree to the terms so we can all get on with the job? What else can you do?"

Joseph growled. "I could kick you in the stomach, strangle you while my two men grab your arms, tie you to a tree, leave you for dead, go hungry for the day, and find the Hoard myself."

Joseph's frustration lent his voice a convincing edge, and for a moment Rook's face lost composure, but even as her eyes went wide with the fear Joseph might actually do those things, her hands did not stray to her knives. Joseph knew then that, thief though she was, she was no fighter. He felt Kaillë's hand on his elbow.

"Joseph," she whispered, "if she'd wanted to harm us, she could have. I won't stand for killing her or leaving her as good as dead, and how else could we keep her from following? Better to let her come along so at least we can watch her and get the supplies back more quickly...isn't it?"

Joseph gave a slight nod. "I just have one more question

for you, Rook" he called. "Why not just keep following us and swoop in at the end to claim your prize?"

"Too many risks," the young woman called back. "I don't know what the endgame will look like, so I can't plan my move. Anyway, your band here almost gave me the slip twice yesterday without trying. You don't leave must trace. I couldn't be sure you wouldn't steal a march on me one night and leave me empty-handed."

"Alright," Joseph said, "you can come along. Know that even if we're led into a trap, I can kill at least one before I fall, and it'll be you."

Rook looked at Kaillë. "Is he always like this?"

Kaillë started at the familiarity in Rook's tone, but quickly recovered. "Yes, actually."

"That's alright," Rook replied, her voice light. "I like a man who broods." She gave Joseph a sly look before she turned to go. "Coming?"

"Tes'oriv," Joseph called. "Stand down." The elf captain and Ten'daren eased out of the trees farther behind Joseph, lowering their bows as they did. At last, Joseph enjoyed a look of unmitigated shock on Rook's face and knew he'd knocked her confidence down a peg. Tes'oriv and Ten'daren had only caught up half a minute before, but Rook didn't need to know that. The hunter smiled. "*Now* we're coming." Joseph set off after Rook, keeping one eye on her and one on Kaillë.

Chapter Five

Rook led the band to a tall elm; up it she had tied their packs, their position invisible from the ground behind a screen of leaves still too stubborn to fall. Joseph had to admit, even with Stitch's nose, if Rook had made efforts to confuse her trail beyond their meeting point, it would have taken them hours to locate the supplies. As it was, Rook had correctly guessed their bearing, and though Joseph's hopes for a hot breakfast were dashed, they were back on their way with no further loss of time.

Joseph called their first halt shortly before mid-day, and Rook collapsed almost before the words left his mouth. Clearly she had neither elven blood nor Joseph's conditioning, not to mention her caper of the previous night, and the sleep it must have cost her, couldn't have helped her endurance. Joseph chuckled at her exhaustion as the rest of the group took their ease and dipped into their water skins and food pouches.

The pert thief was more active during their second halt in the mid-afternoon, and she wasted no time in settling in against a tree trunk across from the tussock on which

Joseph sat.

"So what's your business in all this, hunter?"

"*My* business is just that, thief."

"There's no reason to be unfriendly," Rook admonished. "In fact, if you keep to your end of this deal, when we have a little time I might be persuaded to demonstrate just how *friendly* I can be."

Joseph was abashed, but he endeavored not to show it. He narrowed his eyes "What are you playing at?"

"I'm not playing at anything, yet. Just...setting up the board, so to speak."

"Why?"

"I should have thought that was obvious," Rook purred.

"Pretend that it wasn't."

"Alright. You're tall, strong, and not bad looking...and I can see you have stamina. I'm no thief where men are concerned, but it's clear enough you don't have anything going with the elf maid. Assuming we get the prize with our skins in one piece, why not do some...private celebrating?"

Joseph thought Rook must have been from one of the larger cities to the west. It was said the women were more brazen there. "You're barely more than a child," he said.

"Oh, give me half a chance, and I *know* I can change your mind about that."

Joseph's ideas of propriety ran counter to Rook's proposal, and he felt no specific attraction to her, but he hadn't been with anyone since Delia took ill, and he had certainly never been propositioned so pointedly. His heart quickened a pace.

Suddenly Rook's eyes flicked to Joseph's left. "Don't worry," she said, "I didn't make any headway. We're still neck and neck, I figure." With that, Rook got up and walked away, and Joseph looked over his shoulder to see Kaillë standing behind hm. In the few days he'd known

Identity & Community 67

Kaillë he'd seen her terrified, exhausted, elated, resolute...but he'd never seen her angry until that moment. Her chin was tilted up and her nostrils flared, her shoulders back and fists clenched. Her clan was a small one and her chieftaincy quite young, but Joseph could think of no human noblewoman who could match her cold bearing as she stood there.

"Kaillë," Joseph hazarded, "I didn't..."

Kaillë silenced him with a look, though her eyes softened when they met his, if only slightly. "Save your explanations, Joseph. I know your character. Even if you had done, you owe me nothing. But that *woman*... She presumes too much on *every* front."

Joseph shrugged. "You wanted to bring her along."

Kaillë huffed and tossed her hair before storming off, leaving Joseph to smirk at her departure. So many years he had lived without company of any kind, much less female company. He looked into the woods to the west. If he headed off now, he could be back to his camp by next midday, strike it, and set up somewhere new where no one would bother him and Windrider elves and thieves and prophecies were only a strange memory. Stitch wandered over and licked Joseph's hand, forcing his head up to be pet. "I know, boy," Joseph whispered. "Somewhere deep down, maybe there's even a little pack animal left in me, too."

~ * ~

It was early evening when Joseph and Ten'sael both began noticing signs of Master Aglar and his band of scouts. The enemy had made good progress, but their tracks showed they had also wandered from time to time seeking easier paths. Joseph reconstructed their movements in his mind's eye and could see their craft was good, good enough in fact that he couldn't be sure of their number, though it was certainly larger they he'd hoped; they simply didn't know this forest as his band did. It was an advantage he would need to press for all it was worth. They sped on past sunset as long as they could, but fresh clouds rolled in and hid the moon, forcing a halt for the night.

"We're almost there," Kaillë told Joseph as they prepared their cold camp.

"We'll head in before dawn," he answered, "try to find out where the Hoard could be first and foremost before the rest of the players show up to the party. Stay by my side, no matter what. Even if the Hoard isn't real or isn't there, our enemies believe it is, so there's danger, and I don't want to think of what turns Rook might play as we come to the end."

Kaillë flushed at the mention of the girl's name and began to turn away, but stopped. "Joseph," she said, not looking all the way back to him, "when Rook... Did you consider, I mean, is she...?"

"Kaillë, what is it you really want to ask me?" Joseph interrupted.

She turned fully back to him, suddenly regaining the composure of a proper elf. "I wondered whether you considered me pleasing to look upon."

"I do," Joseph replied easily, counting on her elven nature not to read so much into his reply as a human maid might.

"Thank you," Kaillë answered, as though that cleared the matter entirely, and perhaps it did. "I would like to invoke a blessing over the warriors tomorrow before we go into the village, if that would be alright."

"Of course."

"Good night, Joseph." She walked away, and Joseph spread out his bedroll to sleep.

Identity & Community

~ * ~

Joseph slept but lightly, as was his custom, and guessed it to be an hour too soon for Ten'vahlë to wake him for his turn at watch when he felt a subtle warmth and sense of nearness on his left side. No sound betrayed the sneak's approach, and what little breeze there was carried any scent away, not toward. Something lifted the edge of his blanket. "Whatever you're after," he murmured, "you won't get it." As he spoke, he grabbed the wrist attached to the hand brushing his side.

"Damn," Rook hissed, pulling away.

"Trouble?" Ten'vahlë whispered from his post.

"Nothing, Ten'vahlë, it's fine," Joseph replied as he sat up. "I don't know anything about seduction," he continued to Rook, "but it seems if your goal is to search through a man's cloak, you ought to get him out of it first. Not to mention offering yourself before the venture is over."

"Don't be disgusting," Rook protested. "Call me what you want, I do have a scruple or two left. My offer to bed you was completely sincere."

"Then if that's still for later," Joseph reasoned, "why are you here now?"

"I...thought you might have some other clues about the Hoard."

"Well, I haven't. I would have thought you'd spied on me enough to know that."

"I can only hear what you tell them. Elves are given to strange behavior, but I figured you must have your own agenda."

"Sorry to disappoint you."

"Oh, I'm sure you won't disappoint me when the time comes."

"Go to sleep, Rook. Dawn comes early."

She sneaked off to her place as Joseph rose to relieve

Ten'vahlë. He was awake now, anyway; might as well let the elf sleep.

~ * ~

Proper dawn, in fact, came late, as it always did so close to the mountains' western slopes, but as soon as it was light enough to see, the band was on its feet and ready to depart. They huddled in a knot with Kaillë at its center, her hands held palms forward at chest height. Joseph didn't understand the entire run of ceremonial Elven she spoke, but he caught the phrases for 'clear eyes', 'sharp ears', and 'spirits of light'. When she finished speaking, the elves did seem calmer, and she nodded once to Joseph. With that, they set out.

In less than half an hour, they had hiked eastward into a deep cutting between higher peaks and reached the steep hills surrounding the village of the Windrider clan. Only one break in their encircling arms allowed easy entry; the village lay in a shallow bowl with a forested mountain slope on its north side and the outcrops and ridges of the hills protecting most of the rest. Tes'oriv took the lead, following familiar paths straight back to the road that led through the hills and into the village.

Joseph could see by their clenched jaws and straight backs the elves were trying to steel themselves for what lay ahead, but for all their resolve, half of them wept silently when they passed through the defile and saw what was left of their homes.

The village was in a worse state than Joseph had expected. Structures, both those built into the trees and those on the ground, had been burned. Owing to the damp season, most had not been totally lost to the flames, and their broken shells lay open to the elements through a torched roof here, a collapsed wall there. The storms of two days before had quenched whatever smolders must have remained, leaving only scorched, sodden debris wherever the elves turned their eyes.

Far worse than the wreckage of their homes were the bodies scattered throughout the ruins and across the village green. Some were warriors who had been cut down in a final stand, but many, even most, were those too slow to get away: the infirm, the old...the very young and their parents who wouldn't abandon them. Joseph had seen such butchery during the wars, but still it made his heart sick to see it again, and he was even moved to offer a quick, silent prayer of peace to the spirits of the fallen. The elves, not so inured, stood rooted to their places, unable for a moment to move forward into the carnage.

Joseph's ire at the Baron flamed anew; with ease he could imagine the elven children laughing and playing across the green, but instead they lay silent and broken in their own bloodstains, their once-loving home now a charnel house that would never fully recover from the evil that was done to it. It was true Joseph did not easily live in brotherhood and communion with others, but he had no scorn for those who did, even envied them in rare moments of loneliness. That such a place could be so callously destroyed made his chest tight with anger, so much that in a way he was glad he hadn't seen the carnage when it was fresh. If he had, he would almost certainly have slain the Baron Turov in his fortress, or Master Aglar two nights later, and likely gotten himself killed and a lot of Windriders captured in the process.

The elves still stood immobile, and even Rook had a hand to her mouth in shock over the slaughter before them. "Come on," Joseph said into the silence, his breath showing and disappearing like frosty ghosts as he spoke. "We need to move."

"Should we split up?" Tes'oriv asked. "We could search

more quickly."

"Too dangerous," Joseph answered. "The enemy could show up at any moment, or could be here already. Where should we start?" He was looking at Kaillë.

The elf shook her head. "I told you before, Joseph, I have no idea."

"Are there any ancient ruins in the area?" Rook asked. "Any old cairns, or a cave maybe"

"Only the Greenmound, I suppose. I don't know if it is old as you mean, but it has been there for as long as the Windriders remember. But it's a natural feature, nothing more."

"Show us," Joseph ordered.

Kaillë started to move forward, but Tes'oriv and Ten'sael hastened take point. The rest followed behind, noiseless in their going. They proceeded across the village green, picking their way through the destruction toward the forest fringes on the north side where, standing apart from the denser trees of the wood, a number of trunks thrust up from the earth in what appeared a perfect circle, describing an open space perhaps a hundred feet across, still too deep in shadow for its contents to be known.

The wind shifted, and Joseph's nostrils flared in response to a new scent, the smell of smoke and torn earth. He held up his hand, signaling the band to halt. He was about to reach forward to stop the elves ahead of him, but they held back on their own, either catching the scent or sensing the pause of the group behind them.

A voice ground out from the shadowy clearing. "On your feet! The sun is up; get back to work. I want that slab removed immediately."

Kaillë's breath caught. "It's the Baron," she whispered.

"Attack?" Tes'oriv asked.

Still burning from the carnage around him, Joseph was tempted to give the order, but he had no idea of the enemy's

Identity & Community 73

strength. As the clank of tools issued from the clearing, Joseph looked about for the closest cover, then clenched his teeth to realize he was not the only one doing so. A band of more than a dozen men crept through the village, led by the shaggy-headed form of Aglar, distinct even in the dim light. Joseph's squad was in the open; there was no way they hadn't been seen, and they were outnumbered two-to-one, or worse if Aglar had men Joseph hadn't seen.

"Cottage to the left, cover, go!" Joseph hissed, urging the group toward at least momentary safety. He saw a few of the enemy readying bows, so he loosed three shafts in lightning succession to keep their heads down, but he shot quickly and didn't see any of his arrows strike true before joining the elves behind the husk of the burned-out cottage.

"Now what?" Rook demanded. Her hands trembled, and Joseph was surer than ever she had never seen battle.

"Rook, Ten'sael, stay out of sight and get into that clearing. I want to know what the Baron is up to and how many men he has to be up to it with."

The two slight forms melted into the shadows as the sounds of metal ringing on stone pealed through the razed village. Joseph chanced a look around the corner of the cottage and saw Aglar and his men had sought cover as well. "He doesn't know our number," Joseph whispered to Kaillë. "Likely he thinks we're some of the Baron's lackeys."

"Turov," Aglar shouted as the sun broke over the peaks and dappled the valley with light. "You were holding out on me, Baron. I've caught your sentries napping. What say we talk terms?"

"*You* broke with *me*, Aglar," the Baron's voice shouted back. "You're paid for the work you've done, and I don't know that I need any further. What can you offer to open parlay?" The sounds of heavy labor continued to echo from the clearing.

"He's stalling," Joseph whispered to the elves. "He must be close to his prize, or thinks he is."

"We are between the owl and the mouse, here, Joseph," Tes'oriv stated. "This is not a safe path to be on."

Joseph nodded to the lieutenant, but he had no idea of his next move. If the Baron was close to some artifact of Dalviir, Joseph would go to any length to deny it to him or Aglar, even at the cost of his own life. Still, charging in against foes of unknown strength and disposition was of no help to anyone. Aglar and Turov continued to volley words back and forth over the elves' heads.

Suddenly Ten'sael was among them again, speaking quickly in Elven. His words were too fast and breathless for Joseph's unpracticed ear; he looked to Tes'oriv for translation. "The Baron has some fifty men," the elf explained, "mostly workers, some fighters, some maybe both. They're trying to pry a heavy slab loose from the side of the Greenmound."

"Where's Rook?" Joseph asked.

Ten'sael didn't answer, but looked down with a shameful expression.

"You lost her?" Joseph hissed.

The elf nodded.

Suddenly a heavy boom smote the morning air. The Baron's men must have tipped the slab free. The Baron's voice cut off abruptly, then a flurry of noise erupted from the clearing: people moving, jostling, grabbing tools or weapons. Aglar called once more to the Baron but received no answer. The mercenary captain was sure to charge at any moment.

Chapter Six

"Go," Joseph ordered, pointing to the right. "Stay low, sweep around, get to the clearing. You, too," he added to Stitch, still pointing. The men moved with the dog following closely, but Kaillë hesitated when Joseph stayed still except to draw an arrow. "Go with Tes'oriv," Joseph commanded. "Now!"

The elven lieutenant pulled his chieftain away as Joseph leaned out and stretched his bow. Aglar had just ordered his men out of cover; his great sword was sheathed on his back, exchanged for a large shield and hand ax. He used the shield well, denying Joseph a quick shot. One of the archers had spotted the elves breaking cover and turned in their direction. Joseph loosed his bow. The arrow struck a few inches low, ripping through the archer's cheek and grating into his inner jaw; he dropped his bow and doubled over, screaming and gagging. Joseph loosed a second shaft that took another archer in the left shoulder. The rest of the bowmen then spotted him, redirecting their aim to Joseph's hiding place. He ducked out of the way just as arrows hissed past the corner of his cover. The enemy shafts were right on target and only a split second too late. No more shots followed; they were waiting for him to appear, not wasting undisciplined arrows. These archers were good.

Joseph ran after the elves, weaving as he left cover in case the enemy spotted him again. Just then, a squad of the Baron's men charged out of the circle of trees, demanding all the attention of Aglar's archers.

Joseph caught up to the elves, and together they broke through the circle of trees and brush into the clearing. Joseph could see the Greenmound, at least originally, had been just that, a grassy dome of earth about six feet high at the center, surrounded by tall, straight aspens. Now, however, large swaths of the mound had been stripped of the covering layer of turf to expose bald stone beneath, a smooth, black mineral not natural to the region. In their arcing route to avoid the clash of arms, the elves had entered the circle from the west. To their right, pointing due south, Joseph saw the slab that had been uncovered and removed from the stone mound, but the curve of the dome hid whatever might be inside.

There was no time to ponder the contents or begin to scout them, for no sooner had the band entered the clearing than a gang of the Baron's workers charged them, yelling battle cries, from the north side of the mound. They were armed with a motley assortment of pickaxes, knives, and pry bars, but there were half a dozen of them, all burly and long-limbed. Stitch ran away from the noise back to the safety of the trees, then looked back as if wondering why the rest of the pack wasn't following him. Joseph shoved Ten'daren toward Kaillë, hoping it would be obvious he meant the elf to protect his chieftain. He drew his long knife and turned to face the foe only an instant before the clash. A worker swung a pry bar at him like a mace, but he jumped back at the last moment. The wild swing took his enemy off balance, and he lunged at the man's exposed

Identity & Community 77

flank, punching the knife between his ribs. The man's eyes went wide with shock as Joseph ripped his knife free and shoved him down. Ten'sael had been bull-rushed to the ground, his opponent now kneeling atop him with a pickax raised above his head; Joseph wrapped his left arm around the man's elbows from behind and slit his throat before he could strike. Tes'oriv and Ten'vahlë had felled one enemy and had another at bay, but the two remaining foes were closing in on them from behind. Joseph grabbed the fallen pickax from his last kill, as much for effect as anything, and leapt before the two men, bellowing and swinging the pickax like a scythe. Suddenly forced to engage an enemy that matched their size and clearly beggared their skill, the two men retreated up the mound, leaving the pair of elves to finish their work as Ten'sael regained his feet and weapon.

"Joseph!" Kaillë screamed from behind them. A pair of footmen had thrown Ten'daren to the ground and now were menacing the maid with short swords. The enemy fighters followed Kaillë's gaze and spotted the threat behind them, and the larger of the two grabbed Kaillë and whirled her around in front of him, her feet kicking the air, and used her for what little cover her form provided.

"Drop your weapons or-"

The man crumpled to the ground, dead, with Joseph's knife sticking out from his left eye socket. The remaining soldier growled and charged, heedless of the danger, but managed only two steps before he fell with a pair of elven arrows in his chest. Ten'daren jumped to his feet, his eyes stormy with frustration over his failure, but Joseph had little inclination and less time to salve his conscience. He rallied the band and handed Kaillë the short sword that had been held to her throat only a moment before.

"I don't know how..." she began.

"I know," Joseph reassured, "just hold the sharp end

forward and look mad."

The sounds of fighting from the south grew closer, and Joseph looked to see the Baron's men falling back in a holding action against Aglar's less numerous but more capable fighters. He then heard shouting from the top of the Greenmound as the two men who had retreated from him earlier raised the alarm to their allies on the other side of the clearing. Joseph pointed to them, and Tes'oriv and Ten'vahlë silenced them with arrows, though perhaps too late.

"Should we take the Greenmound, Joseph?" Tes'oriv asked. "We could shoot well from the higher ground."

"No cover up there," Joseph responded above the clash of steel to the south. "Aglar's archers could pick us off from outside the ring of trees. What we really need is to get inside-"

Suddenly a blinding ray of white light poured out of the opening in the Greenmound, giving pause to everyone except the squad of fighters charging over the crest of the mound and down toward Joseph. The hunter took point against them with Ten'sael and Ten'daren while the remaining warriors stood to either side and a pace behind to thin out the enemy ranks with their bows. Kaillë sheltered inside the resulting wedge. Tes'oriv and Ten'vahlë did their work well, and only four men remained by the time they reached Joseph and his elves.

"Third team," the Baron's voice rumbled out from the entrance to the Greenmound, "hold those elves at bay. Everyone else, rally to me."

Joseph was too preoccupied by the foes in front of him to see which way the Baron went, but more than a score of men swept by, ignoring him, as he and the elves fought off the remaining rearguard. They were well trained and had the advantage in size and arms, but Joseph had only to hold them for a moment before Tes'oriv and Ten'vahlë dropped their bows and drew their blades, then the enemy was dragged down and dispatched in short order. The last foe had worked inside Joseph's reach and sought to grapple with him, but Joseph braced his feet and shoved the man back. He was about to drive forward when the enemy's eyes went wide with shock and pain, his mouth working in gasping coughs as he fell forward. Rook stood behind him, her eyes just as wide, with one knife in her hand and the other in the back of the man now dead at Joseph's feet. Suddenly everything was quiet around the Greenmound, the sounds of battle falling to the sounds of chase that receded to the north as the band stood with heaving chests and Joseph marveled, as he had so many times during the war, at how such a brief exertion could leave him so exhausted when his life was at stake.

The band slowly regained their breath, and Joseph was relieved to see that apart from a nasty cut over Ten'daren's eye and a trifling slice on Ten'sael's upper arm, they were unhurt. Kaillë was already reaching into her pack to find dressings for the wounds, but Joseph saw Rook hadn't moved, and her breath hadn't slowed. She just stood, staring at the hilt of her dagger sticking straight up from the dead man's back. Joseph reached down and pulled the blade free, then wiped it clean on the man's tunic. He offered the knife hilt-first to Rook. "Thank you, Rook," he said. "He meant to kill me."

"I didn't.... I mean, I thought, but..."

"I know," Joseph said. "It's alright. You did what seemed best at the moment; it happened, and it's over now. Take your dagger."

Rook reached for it, still barely seeing, but then suddenly drew a breath and met Joseph's eyes. "I was in the Greenmound. It wasn't the Hoard, just a...a map. I know where the Baron's headed."

"Good," Joseph said. "Show me."

The rest of the band had heard the conversation, and Kaillë drew close to Joseph as they moved toward the entrance to the mound. "Wouldn't it still be faster to just follow them?" she asked, eyeing Rook from behind as though she mistrusted the thief's judgment.

"In the short run," Joseph answered, "but we already know we can overtake the Baron and Aglar moving overland. They're still too many to fight, so catching them does us no good, but we could simply pass them by, if..."

"If we already know where they're going," Kaillë concluded.

"Exactly," Joseph answered. "Getting there first is still the surest and safest way to deny them the prize. As for right now, we can afford to give them a few minutes' head start, maybe let them think we only chanced to come back to the village and won't follow them."

"That is very clever, Joseph. I have the respect of my people, and great wisdom in our ways, but I should like to learn to be clever as you are. Would you teach me?"

Joseph paused before entering the Greenmound. "That could take a long time, Kaillë."

Her eyes faltered for but a moment before her face regained its elven composure. "And...after this trouble with the Hoard is over, you mean to go back alone to your forest."

Joseph hesitated. Certainly he *had* meant to, but to hear it said so pointedly, suddenly he struggled to confirm it. A few days ago he'd never dreamed of anything else, but the Windriders he'd come to know through their struggles were so decent, so strong, it pained him, to his shock, to say he planned never to see them again. Kaillë looked up at him with eyes so resolute and yet so innocent; he felt guilt at the thought of abandoning her after she'd placed so much trust in him...guilt, and a longing so sudden and deep it frightened him. He started to cast the feeling aside in panic, but courage was too tightly woven into the fabric of Joseph, so that he bristled at the idea of surrendering to any kind of fear, even this. At last he cleared his throat. "Perhaps it would be better to discuss this when we aren't in such a rush."

"Of course," Kaillë answered. She stepped through the post-and-lintel doorway that led into the mound and down the stone steps on the other side, and Joseph ducked his head to follow her.

Once inside, and after his eyes had adjusted to the torchlight within, Joseph saw Rook's claim that the mound contained a map was a startling understatement. What he saw was a detailed relief carved into the black stone of the floor, mountains that thrust up like stalagmites depicting the whole region within a few miles of the Windriders' valley, all scaled down to fit within a circular chamber perhaps thirty feet across. Even the texture of the stone went from rough to smooth at the tree line of the western peaks, and crystals embedded in the dome's ceiling perfectly represented the starry vaults of night.

"Well," Joseph sighed, "this is impressive, magic or not. The style doesn't look familiar, but even from the outside I couldn't have much doubted that Dalviir built this place."

"How's that?" Tes'oriv asked.

"Because it's so perfectly round," Rook answered.

Joseph had her at knifepoint before she could do much more than blink, as threatening now as he had been kind a moment before. "What did you say?" he growled.

"I din't say nuthin'," Rook protested. Fear widened her eyes, and a distinct western accent was suddenly clear in her voice.

"You said, 'Because it's perfectly round,'" Joseph repeated, "as though you knew that was a trait of Dalviir's structures. There is only one way you could know that."

"I'm a treasure hunter," Rook explained, gaining back some small measure of her nerve. "I spend as much time reading old tomes as...."

"No!" Joseph interrupted. "There were no detailed accounts of his monuments; that's partly why scholars believed him a myth. You've been there. You've *seen* the tomb!"

Slowly, Rook nodded.

"Very clever indeed," Kaillë mused.

"Why did you not say so?" Joseph demanded.

Rook's eyes stayed downcast, and she did not speak.

"Because," Kaillë stated, "she's the one who brought the rubbing to the Baron, showing the inscription from Dalviir's sarcophagus. She started all this."

Rook didn't argue, and Joseph knew Kaillë was right. "I may be clever, Kaillë, but you read people far better than I," he said to the elf. He then continued to Rook, "You'd better tell us all you know, and quickly. You have a village full of blood on your hands, and..."

"No," Kaillë interrupted. "She is innocent of my people's blood."

"How can you say that?" Joseph demanded.

"This much I know you *have* seen, Joseph. Twice now you have threatened her, and neither time did her hand stray to her knife. Even now she rubs at blood on her hand that isn't even there, as though it is a stain on her soul, sickening her. This one has never wished to kill an innocent, not even by proxy."

Joseph looked back at Rook, relaxing his knife just slightly. "Is that true?"

"I didn't know what the writing said," Rook answered. "I still don't. Maye if I'd known what bloodshed it would cause... The Baron made a lot of promises for knowledge about Dalviir, but when I came through on my end, he cut me out of the deal and locked me up in his keep. I guess he wanted to keep me alive long enough to verify my information. It took me a long time to work out all the

Identity & Community 83

angles, but I was finally able to escape when the Baron took most of his men to this place and sent the rest out looking for Windrider survivors and their savior of prophecy."

"And then what, you just walked out of there?" Joseph questioned.

Rook finally looked him full in the eye. "*That's* the part of my story you doubt? You know yourself the security after the Baron left wasn't exactly first rate. Turov isn't the toughest or the smartest robber baron I've escaped from."

"Smart enough to double-cross *you*," Joseph pressed.

Rook looked down again, her face flushed.

"That must not happen very often," Kaillë put in. "This treasure must be very important to you for the desire to have blinded you to the risk."

Rook's eyes were hooded as she looked into Kaillë's. "Score of a lifetime."

"Joseph," Tes'oriv piped up, "this takes too long. The enemy gains ground as long as we stay here."

"Alright, Rook," Joseph said. "Time to earn your keep. Tell us what you saw."

"I think I can do better than tell you." She walked to the center of the space, a flat area about a foot across in the middle of a shallow bowl, all representing the valley in which they now stood. "The Baron stood here with the copy of the rubbing and said, 'Dosh tha Dalviir'ed devorlin. Docen shé cre'al aegle set reall segen.' Then he took a knife and cut his hand- ow."

As she spoke, Rook performed these actions as well. She held out her hand and let the blood drip onto the floor.

The moment the drops splashed onto the stone, they were absorbed into the black rock as though it was a sponge, and a blinding radiance from the crystals overhead suddenly illuminated the chamber. As Joseph blinked the dancing motes from his vision, he saw that after the brilliant glow subsided, three of the larger crystals still shone, each casting a pool of light on the floor a few feet to the north and a point west. The pools overlapped one another, and in the exact center, where all three touched, a point of bright white highlighted an otherwise innocuous cleft in the side of a mountain slope. Meanwhile, three lines of text in the ancient language of Dalviir illuminated a patch of the wall directly across from the entrance to the Greenmound.

"We'll have to steal the Baron's translation or try to overhear it if he doesn't write it down," Joseph said, staring at the rune-like letters and trying to reckon the time to their destination and where along the path they might best intercept the Baron.

"No need," Kaillë said. "I can read these characters."

"What?" Joseph and Rook both asked in surprise.

"'Seek the lighted mountain's child in sunset's shadow. The lance of sun at the Hour of Sating shows the lock. An offering of more life's blood serves as the key.' It's actually quite lyrical in the original tongue..."

"How is that possible?" Joseph asked.

"These characters are used in some of our older ceremonial texts. I've learned them since I was a child. Windriders write down very little," Kaillë explained as the runes slowly faded from the wall, "so our written language has only changed very little over the centuries. I don't know much of human history, but apparently my ancestors must have learned their letters during your Fourth Dynasty era or soon after."

"Rook," Joseph said, "did the Baron read those characters? Really read them?"

"I don't think he really can," she replied. "He copied them onto the rubbing from the tomb; I don't think he can translate them in his head."

"Then he's going the wrong way," Kaillë said, finishing Joseph's thought. "He'll make for the mountain that was lit,

Identity & Community 85

but the verse said to seek the lighted mountain's *child* in the sunset's shadow. With light from the west, the shadow would fall east. Look there," she said, pointing, her voice quickening with excitement. "To the east of the large mountain, that smaller peak. There's even a cleft in the side like on the larger one."

"And not a natural one, I'll wager," Joseph added. "You're right, Kaillë. Aglar and the Baron will be a quarter of the way up the higher slope by the time they stop to rest long enough for the Baron to make his translation. Then he'll have to find a way back down that doesn't take him straight through Aglar's warriors. Rook, was there anything else?"

"No. The Baron studied the light on the map, copied the characters from the wall, then ran out and rallied his men to head east."

"Alright. I hope everyone's rested enough. We're moving out."

Chapter Seven

After liberating what useful supplies and tools they could from the Baron's abandoned camp, Joseph's party headed to the north and a point east, making for the smaller slope the ancient verse had indicated. The ascent was slow and steep, and within an hour they had left the lower, forested reaches and had only low scrub and boulders for cover. After another hour Joseph called a brief halt; the final ascent to the mountain cleft was within easy reach, and the Baron's men could be seen across the dividing valley, still laboring up the wrong slope. Aglar's band was following at a deliberate pace, not tiring themselves. "Aglar probably plans to let the Baron find the prize and then simply take it from him," Joseph said for the benefit of the Windriders who might not anticipate the ploys of human cutthroats. "If they knew what Dalviir's artifacts were capable of, they wouldn't be so cavalier about letting the Baron lay hands on them."

"Joseph," Rook said from behind him. Her voice was low and more timid than Joseph had imagined she could muster. "I know how much damage these treasures might

Identity & Community

do, and... I just... I do have a conscience; there are things I won't do for this prize, and I won't let anything so terrible fall into evil hands. I know you won't believe me, but I had to say it, anyway."

She turned and walked away then without a quip or flirtation, and by that alone Joseph was forced to believe her sincerity, his weaknesses at reading people notwithstanding. Still, Joseph was less concerned with Rook's intentions than with her actions, and even were that not the case, her declaration changed nothing of the matter at hand, so Joseph spoke again to Kaillë, asking if she knew the meaning of "the Hour of Sating".

"I'm uncertain," the elf replied, "but I believe it refers to the hour after the morning meal, when you are sated after breaking your fast."

"But the clue referenced 'the lance of the sun,'" Joseph rebutted. "Early in the day, as Dalviir would have reckoned it, this slope will still be in shadow."

"Not the morning meal," Rook said suddenly, "the midday meal. It's true the old books have little enough to say about Dalviir's monuments, but they say plenty about the time when he lived. During the Fourth Dynasty, meals at morning and evening were small; only the midday meal really sated."

"So we're looking for the lance of the sun an hour after high noon, then?" Kaillë clarified.

Rook shrugged. "Unless someone has a better idea."

Joseph eyed the sun and the distance to the cleft. "We'd best get moving. If Rook is right, the Hour of Sating is only a couple of hours away. We won't get another chance until tomorrow, and by then the Baron will have caught up and chased us off...or cut all our throats."

The band set out again, heading up the final, steepest slope as quickly as they could. They were fortunate no true scaling was required; as Tes'oriv and Ten'daren went forward, being the most surefooted, they found a subtle path cutting back and forth across the slope. Even still, it ran quite steep at times, so they were forced to take it in turns being the first to scrabble up the slope and then let down a rope to assist the rest, lest they exhaust themselves completely in the ascent. Stitch proved to be a decent climber, but one of the slopes was too steep even for him, forcing Joseph to carry the dog as he fought up the rock with the rest hauling from above. The going was slow, and Joseph watched the sun climb to its zenith with growing concern. His anxieties were to find no comfort when Ten'vahlë called for Tes'oriv's attention in Elven. Tes'oriv spoke to Joseph a moment after.

"Joseph, look to the larger peak. The enemy stirs."

Joseph did as Tes'oriv bid him and saw the Baron and a cadre of guards had moved back down the larger mountain toward the tree line. For all the chasing around over the last few days, it was the first time he'd had a proper look at Baron Turov. The man was tall, of average build, and well-dressed in purple. He was too far away to make out his face, but his hair was black and trimmed close. Emerging from the trees farther down the slope came Aglar, also under guard, and unless Joseph missed his guess, Gren, Turov's erstwhile master at arms, accompanied Aglar as well.

"Damn," Joseph cursed. "Our best hope was that they would kill each other. Not much chance of that now."

"Even if they come to an agreement," Kaillë pointed out, "surely neither of those men could be trusted to honor it."

"Honor has nothing to do with it," Joseph spat. "Turov will be slaughtered if he doesn't call the truce, and as long as he's just smart enough to keep his translation of the runes to himself, Aglar has no hope of getting the treasure without him. That will keep their uneasy alliance secure until they reach the Hoard, and by then they'll have gone right through us if we don't get there first."

The band redoubled their efforts, and with only minutes to spare they filed into the cleft, a rough, three-sided shaft running all the way to the mountain's peak. The view of blue sky at the top of the shaft was obscured by a crystal lens that painted a fist-sized spot of light on the cleft's floor. "That should be the spot then," Joseph said, "for offering the blood. Right? Or at least it will be in a minute or two."

"I went last time," Rook said, fingering the bandage wrapped around her left hand.

After waiting what felt like the appropriate time, Joseph rolled up his sleeve, taking his knife to the back of his left forearm. The party looked on with tense anticipation as he let the blood run down the back of his hand and drip off his fingertips onto the stone.

Nothing happened.

"Dammit!" Joseph cried. He stepped out of the cleft to look across at the motion of the brush on the opposite slope, wondering whether he should take the band back down the mountain before they were trapped in the cleft by a force of some forty warriors. Rook's guess had seemed good, but since it had failed, they had no idea when to try next. There wasn't time to wait around dropping blood on the ground every few minutes, and even if there was, who could know what traps Dalviir might have left behind, triggered by blood in the wrong location? They may have only been very lucky to escape unscathed after guessing wrong the first time.

"Wait," Kaillë said. "Joseph, the stars. The crystals, I mean, in the ceiling of the Greenmound. What season did they show?"

Joseph closed his eyes and thought back, remembering the three brightest crystals in particular, which certainly matched the three brightest stars in the sky. "High summer," he replied. "I'm sure of it."

"So the sun should be higher..."

Joseph jumped back into the cleft, looking up at the crystal lens above and imaging the sun's position at an hour after noon on midsummer's day. He took a pair of steps back from the spot of light on the cleft floor and squeezed more blood from the wound on his arm, holding his breath as the drops fell to the stone.

A deep rumble sounded as the blood disappeared into the rock, and a section of the back wall of the cleft swung inward like a great, stone door. Joseph looked up at Kaillë. "Pretty clever yourself, chieftain."

The elf smiled as the band moved through the doorway, Joseph taking point. The sunlight seeped only dimly through the narrow door, so Tes'oriv stepped back into the light to dig a torch from his pack and set it alight. As he ducked back inside they prepared their minds for whatever wonders or horrors Dalviir had left in store for them. The torchlight flickered into the darkness, bouncing off the gleaming, black stone walls that lined the interior, driving back the shadows to reveal everything within.

The chamber was empty. Twelve stone plinths stood up from the floor, making a circle around the room about a foot from the wall, but no treasures stood atop them.

Rook cursed and punched the wall, and Joseph turned in surprise at her outburst.

"What does this mean?" Kaillë asked. "There is no Hoard, and never was?"

"Then why the map room, and the clues in his tomb?" Joseph reasoned. "Why go to all the trouble? From all I know of Dalviir, he was dangerously mad, but not a foolish prankster."

"Of course there was a Hoard!" Rook shouted. "Don't you fools see what's happened? Somebody got here first. Maybe by a hundred years! The treasure is long gone, and all this was for nothing. All of it!" She looked at the surrounding elves with pain in her bloodshot eyes.

Identity & Community 91

"That doesn't track, either," Joseph said, keeping his head. "King Ludvarch fought...well, not the whole war, but by all accounts a major campaign just to get close enough to a rumored location of Dalviir's tomb to sneak a team in to investigate. If the Hoard had really been discovered, the continent would have been at war over control of the treasures, to say nothing of all the deaths or miracles, or both, the artifacts themselves would have caused. It isn't the kind of thing that could stay secret for long if it was out in the world."

"What are you suggesting?" Kaillë asked.

"I'm not sure yet." Joseph paced back to the door and set his shoulder against the stone slab. His feet slid across the smooth floor and his lean muscle strained, but the stone stood firm. Convinced nobody could have entered by that way previously without leaving the door standing open, Joseph paced the edges of the room and, stooping low with the torch, sought any evidence of tampering. "Here," he said at last. "Bring tools."

Tes'oriv and Ten'daren came closer with pry bars, Rook trailing only slightly behind to watch. Joseph had pulled a corner of his cloak forward and was brushing at a hairline crack in the stone that ran in a half circle on the floor against the back wall of the chamber.

"This room *has* been entered before," Joseph affirmed, "just not by the front door. And by the precision of the stonework, I can say who by: dwarves."

The elves chuckled, but Kaillë's face went stern. "Joseph," she said, "I appreciate you trying to lighten the mood, especially since it doesn't come naturally for you, but now is really no time for jokes."

Joseph looked over his shoulder and met her eyes, uncomprehending.

"No, I'm sure he's right," Tes'oriv replied, still smiling. "Stocky men who live their whole lives without ever seeing the sky just tunneled through the solid rock and took the treasure." He laughed again, his sarcasm obvious even through his accent.

"I don't see what's funny," Joseph insisted, aggravation equally obvious in his tone.

"Come, Joseph, be serious," Kaillë said. "Dwarves aren't real."

Joseph looked at Rook, his eyes beseeching. "Don't look at me, hunter," she said. "I'm just a city girl from the western plains. I can't say *what* you mountain folk see when you're drinking."

Joseph looked back at Kaillë. "You don't believe in dwarves," he said flatly.

"Of course not, and neither should you. I gather you've had some prior contact with my people by how quickly you've started learning our language, but I think someone must have been having a joke at your expense. Dwarves are just stories for small children, what humans might call 'bogeymen.' You know, 'Do all your chores or the dwarves will come at night and drag you down to their mines, where you'll have to work forever and never see the sun and stars again.' None but the smallest children actually believe it. No offense," she added quickly in response to Joseph's scowl.

"Well," the hunter replied, "I had crossed paths with elves, but they never told me a whit about dwarves. Humans have had run-ins with them from time to time over the centuries, sometimes friendly, sometimes not so friendly. I suppose some of the city folk might have started wondering if they're just legends, but I know better. Personally."

Chapter Eight

Nine years earlier...

Joseph was wet, cold, hungry, and exhausted after spending most of the day fleeing from a battle that had ended in disaster. He and his men had scouted the enemy position and made a clean escape. The problem with war was sometimes all the advance knowledge of your enemy just wasn't good enough. There were factors of numbers, arms, the strength of a key unit's courage, all of which were beyond Joseph's control.

The infantry had moved forward to engage the enemy, protecting the flanks of a cavalry charge. The horsemen were led by Sir Walter of Dunworth, as arrogant a noble as Joseph had met, but he was a man of honor and would lead his warriors well. Based on the word of Joseph's scouts, the leaders knew a counter-attack would strike the north flank, but they'd counted on the infantry to hold long enough for the cavalry to break the main lines and redeploy. They didn't.

Joseph and his scouts, their work finished for the day, had been on a hill more than a strong bowshot away, watching the battle among the supply wagons and camp followers. He saw the left flank start to waver, crack, dissolve, and watched the enemy overwhelm their cavalry from the rear and roll up the right flank like an old rug. Sir Walter tried to rally his men to break free and reach safety, but it was no use.

Most of the people around Joseph had fled as soon as the battle turned. Joseph's men were also not of the 'stand or die' mentality any more than he was, so he'd led them into the nearby foothills in the hopes of skirting the enemy picket lines and reaching the larger post of friendly forces to the south. The enemy patrols were thicker than he'd hoped, and they'd found themselves forced ever eastward and upward to avoid detection. The weather had turned two hours before nightfall and sent their situation from bad to worse.

Finally one of Joseph's scouts spotted a cave in the deepening gloom, and, seeing no sign of bats or large predators, Joseph led his men inside. He wasn't taking the first watch, so he spread out his wet cloak to dry and stretched out on the cold stone to sleep, using his pack for a pillow. He wondered as he listened to the rain outside the cave whether it rained over his home as well. Was Delia just laying down to sleep, as he was, or had she retired early? As he shifted his head to stop his spade from jabbing behind his ear through the canvas of his pack, he wondered if she'd been at work in the garden that day. Winter was fast approaching; did she have enough stored up to weather it? He fought to set his worry aside. She'd had eight months since his departure to prepare for the snows; all he could do for her now was end this war quickly so he could return.

He slept more deeply than was his custom and woke with a start when Nathan, his youngest but cagiest man, came to wake him for his watch. Joseph rubbed the sleep from his eyes, learned Nathan had nothing to report, and went to the entrance of the cave to stand sentinel. His watch passed without incident, and in an hour he was back to sleep and dreaming of home. Klaus, his second, woke him an hour before daylight.

"Captain, the enemy is up early and on the move. They're sure to pass by here within the hour. What are your orders?"

Joseph cursed as he sat up. If he moved his men out immediately, they could avoid detection for a time, maybe long enough, but they were bone weary, hungry and thirsty; supplies were low, and they couldn't hope to forage while on the run. If they stayed put until the enemy passed, they could take time to see to their needs, but the odds of detection were high if the enemy sent out skirmishers, which was likely in the aftermath of yesterday's battle.

"Make a light," Joseph said. "Take Nathan and scout the back of the cave. If it goes deep enough, we should be able to hide in the darkness until they're gone. I doubt their scouts will do more than look in the entrance."

Joseph watched the pair move deeper into the cave, taking a turn around a rock outcrop so only the glow of their torch on the back wall could be seen. So far, so good, Joseph thought. "Alright, men," he quietly instructed. "Gather your gear and prepare to move deeper into the cave. Wipe clean every trace that we were..."

Suddenly a cry echoed from the depths of the cave, and the flickering reflection of the torchlight winked out.

"Thatcher, Donald, with me; Ulf, Tobias, hide our gear and follow." With that, Joseph rushed forward to see what had befallen his men. A light sprang up behind him as Thatcher or Donald lit another torch, casting Joseph's shadow before him as he ran. He had his long knife drawn as he rounded the corner, prepared for anything, or so, at least, he thought. He stopped short at the empty stretch of tunnel before his eyes, Thatcher and Donald drawing up with another couple of steps and doing likewise. There were no enemies, no wild beasts, no pits or rock falls: just a twenty foot stretch of bare tunnel ending in a blank wall of stone. There were no signs of struggle; even Klaus' torch was nowhere to be seen. If Joseph didn't know better, he'd swear he'd only brought four men into the cave instead of six. The suddenness of their disappearance hinted at magic, a force Joseph had no truck with. He'd seen it on the battlefield only once so far, and he was eager never to see it again, though he knew that was unlikely. Still, two men's lives, at least, depended on his courage, so he moved forward with Thatcher and Donald, ordering Ulf and Tobias to stay at the corner to keep watch.

"Thatcher," he ordered, "light another torch. We need more light to inves-" A rush of air no louder than a whisper breathed past as three spans of stone flew inward, creating three doors where before had been only rock. Before even Joseph could react, and with Thatcher's right arm still elbow deep in his pack digging for a flint, Joseph, Thatcher, and Donald were surrounded by a ring of spear points held by short, dense men whose skin, hair, and clothing blended perfectly with the browns and grays of the stone around them. Barely as tall as Joseph's armpit but with shoulders the breadth of a large man, they stood immobile, so still they might have been statues but for the twinkles of their all-black eyes in the light of Donald's torch.

One of the men spoke, but Joseph saw no distinguishing marks of rank or authority. "Order your two remaining men into the circle or you die, and they will fall soon after."

Joseph couldn't afford to test their resolve or determine if they might be bluffing. If these dwarves, for so he was sure they must be, didn't like his answer, he'd be impaled before he could move, and Delia would never even know his fate. He gave the order.

"You are the leader, then?" the dwarf speaker asked as

Ulf and Tobias shouldered their way through the hedge of spears.

Ulf caught Joseph's eye and glanced toward the dwarf to his left, but Joseph warned him to stand down with a tight shake of his head. "I'm the leader," he answered the dwarf.

"Your other two men are unharmed, for now," he said. "They refused to speak except to say their leader would speak for them. Then you appeared. Why are you here?"

"I've taken one more order under threat from you than you'd have been wise to make. Stay your spears, and I'll answer your questions."

The dwarf stared deeply into Joseph's eyes, then raised his spear to point straight up. Without a verbal order the other dwarves did the same in perfect unison. "Why are you here?" he repeated.

"What right have you to ask?" Joseph argued. "I see no sign of anyone living here or laying any other claim to it."

The dwarves tensed. "You said..."

"I said I'd answer your questions," Joseph interrupted. "I didn't say I wouldn't ask any of my own."

The dwarf gave him the same piercing look, then nodded once. "Look up. You see not sky, but stone. The dwarves claim dominion of all lands under the land and rights to all goods abandoned therein. This region lies under the control of the Fourteenth Clan, which I am empowered to represent within the boundaries of the Third Patrol. Why are you here?"

"We sought shelter for the night."

"The sun has risen over the surface and the sky's water has stopped falling. Why have you not left?"

"We have enemies abroad," Joseph answered.

"You are fighters in the surface war, then?"

Joseph nodded.

"We want no part of your wars. You must leave

immediately. Your two men will be returned." The dwarves opened their circle on one side, leaving only one clear path – toward the cave's exit.

"If you wanted to kill us, stabbing would have been quicker," Joseph said, unmoving. "You've wasted too much of our time, and the sun is higher. If we can't shelter until the enemy has passed, we'll be seen and killed."

"That is no concern of ours," the dwarf replied.

"It's about to be," Joseph threatened. "I know my men don't stand much chance against the dozen of you, but it's a damn sight better than against the *hundreds* out there. How many good dwarves are you willing to lose chasing us out of a cave you weren't using anyway?"

"...Your proposal is sound. You may remain as an anomaly on our patrol. Two dwarves will remain to guard you. They will not hinder you from moving about or leaving this cave. We will return before concluding our patrol, which will coincide closely with surface nightfall. If you still remain then, you will be forced out."

Without waiting for a reply, the dwarves turned to leave, save two, who kept their places. Again there was no gesture or discussion, nor even any hesitation, two simply stayed while the rest marched away through one of the concealed doors. Nathan and Klaus appeared a moment later, then the door swung shut, leaving no sign the portal had ever been there.

"Quench that light," Joseph ordered. "Ulf, Tobias, bring our gear back here, then keep your ears open. Get comfortable, boys. We need to stay quiet and out of sight for an hour or so, assuming we haven't already been heard in here with all the pointless negotiation."

"We are sorry for that," one of the dwarves said. "You seem like decent folk, but the dhor-zabh is somewhat...strict about regulations."

"'Thorzav,' is that your word for your commander,

then?" Klaus asked, keeping his voice low. Joseph was tempted to order silence, but his curiosity got the better of him. If what he knew of dwarves were arrows, they wouldn't fill a child's quiver, though he'd heard many suspect tales.

"Our patrol does not have a leader as yours does. We are raised together from birth as a hret-d- ah, a 'stonebound' unit. The dhor-zabh is not one of us, it is *all* of us."

Suddenly the perfect coordination of the dwarven troop was eerily clear. "You hear each other's thoughts," Joseph said.

"No," the dwarf replied, "not as you would imagine it. It begins that way, when we are young, but a fully trained hret-dialt doesn't hear thoughts so much as share in them. From the several, bonded minds springs a mutual consciousness."

"Do you share in it even now?" Nathan asked.

"No. Too much stone in the way now. We share only with one another." The dwarf nodded to his compatriot, who nodded back. "When we are alone we are called Thak and Dirv. We are pleased to be talking with you. We are more curious than our dhor-zabh, and we rarely meet surface-walkers."

"You speak our language perfectly," Klaus noted.

"Yes, and many others. Such learning is easy when twelve minds share in the labor. But tell us of the surface, please. Mostly we want to know, what causes this war?"

"King Ludvarch is a monarch to the northwest," Joseph answered. "His lands are larger than his neighbors', and yet he seeks to grow an empire at their expense. The folk under his rule know no rest or mercy, so his neighbors rise up against him. He is mad in his lust for power. What he cannot possess he destroys. The war has been brutal, and it shows no sign of slowing."

"Even we know this king," the dwarf answered. "In his

own lands he has caused great distress. Rumors come to us from the Seventeenth and Twentieth clans that he sends strange men into the depths of the earth, probing the stone as though searching for something. Twice he has found dwarves. For now we have made sure none survive to report on our homes, but as he sends more men, the battle will grow more difficult."

"It sounds like we have more in common than..." Suddenly a movement at the corner of the tunnel caught Joseph's eye, and he nocked an arrow to his bow. A shadow flitted away, and Joseph sprang to his feet to give chase. Ulf and Tobias turned and drew arrows as well, their actions rushed with the embarrassment of having been surveilled unawares. As the three archers rounded the corner, they saw a figure silhouetted against the morning light of the cave mouth, sprinting away. "Stop," Joseph shouted. "We'll shoot!" The figure kept fleeing. Joseph bent his bow, followed immediately by his men, and in an instant three arrows had thudded into the silhouette's back. Momentum carried the shape forward as it fell, and Joseph rushed ahead to watch as the spy tumbled out of the cave and down the rocky hillside below, dragging loose small stones that rattled down the slope, their echoes rebounding throughout the foothills.

At the bottom of the hill, Joseph saw the body slide to a stop...at the foot of a skirmish force of twenty men wearing Ludvarch's insignia. The drums of a full marching column reached him faintly on the wind. Joseph stood in shadow, but the leader of the enemy unit pointed up toward the cave mouth and muttered orders, and three scouts began their ascent toward Joseph's position. Joseph turned and moved silently back into the cave, waving Ulf and Tobias back around the corner to the rest of the men.

"We're in trouble," he hissed to them. "Scouts inbound; even if we kill them, the cave's been spotted, so we'll have more company when they don't come back."

The dwarves looked briefly at one another, then one spoke. "We will hide you." He moved to a place on the tunnel wall next to one of the hidden doors and pressed for a moment, then the door swung open. The remaining dwarf ushered Joseph and his men inside, then the door was shut behind them, plunging Joseph into total darkness.

"You will be quite safe here," the dwarf declared. "They will not hear us through the heavy stone of our doors, and they will not find them for any length of searching."

"Thank you," Joseph whispered into the darkness. "I believe the enemy only saw the body at the end of its fall; when they find the cave empty, they're likely to believe we shot from the hilltop above and move on."

Joseph expected the dwarves to kindle a light, but after a few moments he realized he, a 'surface-walker', was probably not meant to see the domain of the dwarves. "If you want to make a light," Joseph said, "my men and I will consent to be blindfolded. We are in your debt, and there's no need for all of us to be blind."

"There is no need for light," the dwarf replied. "We enjoy it at times and use it for precise work in our crafts, but when it is lacking we see well enough with our ears, as bats do. That's why we run them out of our surface outposts. All their screeching as they come and go is very alarming."

Joseph didn't understand what they said about seeing with their ears, nor about bats doing the same, but he chose not to press for further explanation.

As they sat waiting to be confident the enemy had gone, the dwarves continued to ask questions, though only one ever spoke, and as the final tensions eased between the two patrols, they even answered a few of their own. Finally, they asked Joseph where he and his men were going.

"There is an outpost of our people to the south," Joseph explained. "It's a difficult journey, but our division was routed, and there's nowhere nearer that we can find safety. And somehow we need to steal a march on the enemy and make it to the fort in time to warn them that Ludvarch's forces are heading right for them."

Tobias groaned. "You all know what that means. Unless Captain Slavedriver passes out from exhaustion, no sleep for the next three days."

The darkness echoed with chuckles of assent and snorts at Tobias' "softness", then all was silent for a few moments.

"We know this fort," the dwarf said. "There is an exit to the surface near there, in the Fifth Patrol.

"Our roads run straighter and smoother than those above; the exit can be reached in a day. We do not know how long the surface journey from there to your fort, but surely you would save time. We will take you there."

Joseph was about to protest, but the dwarf kept speaking almost as if reading his thoughts. "The dhor-zabh will not be pleased at first, but once we rejoin our hret-dialt, they will know your need as we do and approve our action." Joseph heard the scraping of stone behind him and turned with a start. "Do not worry," the dwarf said, "we are only leaving a stone-sign for our unit to find when they return. We are glad to help you against this mad king Ludvarch, but we insist that you make no light. We will guide you, and we assure you the way is quite safe."

Chapter Nine

Present Day...

"I spent a day in the dwarven realm," Joseph concluded his story, "and never saw so much as a foot of it. But the dwarves were real, I promise you that."

The elves accepted his brief recounting of dwarven life with looks ranging from awe to disgust. "How can they live that way?" Kaillë questioned. "Always in the darkness, never knowing things that grow and thrive in the light and fresh air. It sounds as awful as the stories I heard as a child."

"Well," Joseph answered, setting a chisel against the seam in the stone and pounding it with a wooden mallet, "I suppose they'd think the same of how we live, always under the threat of weather and the changing seasons. Probably seems ridiculous to a dwarf."

Kaillë shuddered. "I suppose so..."

The black stone was uncommonly tough, but after twenty minutes of alternating work, Joseph and the elves had chipped away a large enough pocket for a pry bar to get a bite on. Five minutes more of prying, hauling on ropes, cursing, and skinned knuckles later, a semicircular hole, less than two feet across, stood open before them with the plug of stone upended just next to it. They tried to cast torchlight into the hole, but the aperture was narrow, and the flickering light of the torch would not dispel the shadows.

"Should we just throw the torch down, then?" Rook asked.

"It could be a hundred feet down that hole," Joseph answered, "and if it is, it'd be a waste of a perfectly good torch." He looked around for another solution.

The stone chips they'd made in their work were too small to use as weights, so Joseph tied a rope around the mallet he'd been using and lowered it into the hole to sound the depth, gauging the rope length by his forearm as he paid it out slowly. The rope went slack after only about eight feet.

"You should still throw the torch down next," Rook advised. "Smooth floors stop falling mallets, but so do spikes and scorpions."

Joseph raised his eyebrow. "Scorpions?"

"...Well...not personally, but I've heard stories."

Joseph nodded to Tes'oriv, who dropped his flaming brand into the hole. It flickered a bit as it bounced on the floor but brightened again when it came to rest, showing no danger in the surroundings. Joseph jumped down first, and within a few minutes the whole party was on the floor below, taking their first steps into the underground realm of the dwarves.

"So now what?" Rook asked.

"Now we search for signs of life down here," Joseph said. "The Hoard didn't cut its own way out of that chamber."

"I still say it's been gone for a century. Either way, we're wasting our time down here."

"You're welcome to leave whenever you like," Kaillë

Identity & Community

huffed.

"No..." Rook answered. "I've got to try. I'm seeing this through to the end." Her voice was harder and more ragged than Joseph had heard it before, and he looked back at the girl. He saw by a glance from Kaillë the elf had noticed the change as well, but Rook just shouldered past Joseph and took point without saying anything more.

Joseph touched Kaillë's shoulder, motioning her to hang back. Once Rook and the other elves had moved farther ahead, he bent down to murmur into her ear, lest echoes reach the thief at the head of their party. "Rook is different since we found the empty chamber above. She seems more determined in some ways, but hopeless at the same time. What do you make of it?"

"She has more invested in this quest than she's telling us. I don't know what it is, but this Hoard means something more to her than material gain. I'm sure of it."

Stitch, a few paces ahead, started acting skittish, but Joseph ignored him for the moment and pressed Kaillë. "What could it be, then? Dalviir's artifacts are lethal, and you said yourself she's no killer."

"That's the part I still-"

"Aaaaaaaaaaaaiiiiiiiiie!"

Kaillë's words were cut off by Rook's stone-splitting scream from up the tunnel. Joseph turned and dashed toward the torchlight but only got a few steps before he saw the cause of the girl's terror. Mere paces in front of her in the shadows of the tunnel floated a vicious-looking head, the size of a horse's but with lips pulled back to bare fangs the size of knives jutting both up and down, and from behind them came a low, rumbling snarl. A twinkle of eyes and flash of white fur framed the teeth; everything else was lost to the darkness and horror of the confrontation. The whole party stood stock still, not daring even to twitch, while Stitch bared his teeth in challenge as the hair of his neck and shoulders bristled. Joseph was about to tell Rook to start slowly backing away when a voice boomed from the deeper tunnels, "Steva, easy, boy. What have you found over there?"

The coal-black nose above the teeth made a perfunctory sniff before the lips closed and the beast turned its head toward the voice, revealing a long, lean muzzle of white and black stripes at the front of a stout chest and sturdy legs. It was a badger, Joseph realized, though larger than a pony. A glint close to the floor revealed that the animal's long, broad claws had been tipped with metal, turning them into tiny chisels.

"Who goes there?" the voice called again, and Joseph saw the barest shape of a dwarf at the edge of the torchlight. The badger's posture was no longer threatening, but it stood defensively between the party and its master.

Joseph put his hand on Stitch's head to comfort him and offered him a piece of jerky for his bravery as he answered. "I am Joseph, surface-walker and hunter, and friend to Thak and Dirv of the Fourteenth Clan. These are my people; I will spare introductions for now. We are on urgent business. What clan's lands are these, and who am I talking to?"

The dwarf stepped into the torchlight, revealing a shorter and rangier build than the guards Joseph had met during the war, covered with dusty, leather clothes and topped with a face of dark tan behind a bushy, black beard. Still, he had the same all-black eyes, the same impossibly still posture. "These are the lands of the Ninth Clan, or were, and I am called Dorav the Restless. If this region was still properly patrolled, you'd be at spear point by now. What brings you to the realm of the dwarves against such danger?"

"I would rather tell our tale to someone in charge, Dorav," Joseph replied. "I don't know much of dwarven ways, but I guess that a leader of the clan doesn't call himself 'the Restless'. Am I right?"

"You are. I am a rover; I earn my living finding new tunnels or scouting old ones. Lately I've been mapping this section for the guard. We lost it to trolls during my grandfather's time. We've had it back for years but haven't opened it up yet. If you want to talk to somebody in charge, I'll have to take you back to the city. You can tell the elders what you're doing here. I recommend you just leave instead. The elders have no sense of humor, and if they don't trust your story, you might not like the results. If you go back the way you came now, I can forget I saw you and we can both go about our way."

Joseph suspected Kaillë and the rest of the elves had already been underground longer than they cared to, but he was determined not to go back. "We will take our chances with the elders," Joseph replied. "Lead the way, Dorav. Do you need us to douse our lights?"

"Nah," Dorav grunted. "Those Fourteenth Clan dhorzabhs are too paranoid for their own good. Too many years patrolling too close to a war zone, if you ask me. Steva likes the light, anyhow. Not that his nose isn't sharp enough to follow me, but what's the point in traveling around with a rover if you don't get to see the sights?"

As Steva turned and padded away, Joseph wondered aloud, "Why is it that all the new people I meet lately have giant animals working for them?"

"Why wouldn't they?" Dorav replied, not turning. "Humans do the same."

"I don't know what you've heard," Rook answered, "but humans just ride horses, mostly."

"And are there not smaller versions of those?" Kaillë asked, her voice amused.

Joseph chuckled once. "Fair enough." They walked for a few minutes before Joseph spoke again. "Dorav, you said these lands were lost and that you only reclaimed them a few years ago. Yet you're out here all alone. I would think the enemy lands couldn't be far off."

"Trolls live deep," Dorav replied. "Real deep. Dwarves see to that. They make a successful grab for the surface tunnels now and again, but when we get to tossing 'em back down, we toss 'em *down* deep." Dorav looked over his shoulder and caught Joseph with an impish half-smile. "Real deep."

Joseph smirked. He had to be wary Dorav was more than he seemed, but taking him at face value, he liked the dwarf's demeanor.

The party walked on for over an hour, and Joseph lost all sense of where they were or the way back. A few times the hunter picked at the cut on his left forearm, letting a few drops of blood trickle down in the hopes it would help Stitch sniff their way back out if they had to make a quick exit. Even that contingency was low on his list of priorities. No doubt the Baron and Aglar would follow along their path, so if Joseph couldn't make allies of the dwarven elders, there was likely no way they could make it back to the surface. Joseph glanced back at Kaillë and wondered if she was ready for the challenge. Joseph was no diplomat; it would fall to her to speak for the party to the elders, and Joseph wondered whether she could represent them to a group of people she'd believed were only a fairy story just a few hours before.

The tunnel made a turn, and Joseph caught the faintest noise echoing up from the caverns ahead. There was nothing distinct in it, just a slight "something else" that stood in contrast to the footfalls and breathing that had dominated the last hour. "Getting close, now," Dorav said. "Should be able to see the gates in a little bit."

The sounds grew louder as they progressed, and Joseph was eventually able to understand them as a jumble of voices, cart wheels, peals of hammers and picks, and all the

Identity & Community

other bustle of life and industry one heard in a human city, only distorted by the echoing twist of tunnels between his ears and the source. Another turn of the tunnel, and a glow of light ahead backlit a grating of iron bars and the silhouette of two dwarves holding halberds.

Dorav shouted in dwarven, and the guards stirred. They shouted back, then Dorav replied. After that, he turned to Joseph. "I've asked them to speak your language," he said quietly. "It's rude to talk about you in words you can't understand. You're guests, not prisoners, until the elders decide different."

"Until?" Joseph asked.

Dorav shrugged. "I told you it was better to just go back."

Joseph grimaced, and Rook and Kaillë looked at him with wide, nervous eyes. "Believe it or not," he replied to Dorav, "it wasn't."

One of the guards marched off, and the other called back. "What business do the surface-walkers have in the city?"

"They say it's urgent," Dorav called, "and they've requested to speak to the elders. I hear no deceit in their words. I will vouch for them to appear before the elders under the usual guard."

The first dwarf returned, accompanied by a cadre of warriors, as Joseph and his party reached the gate.

The second guard opened a lock and unbarred the gate. "Your long-legged badger will have to be roped," the guard said. "Our full-sized animals may think he is food if he wanders off."

Joseph looped a harness out of a length of rope and coaxed Stitch's head through it. "He's a dog," Joseph said. A few of the guards snorted. "What?" Joseph demanded.

"In our language, 'dog' means something bad," Dorav explained.

"'Long-legged badger' it is," Joseph said, shaking his head.

They marched forward at the center of a ring of guards, passing side tunnels that grew more frequent as the main tunnel widened. Other dwarves appeared in the thoroughfare in increasing numbers, all looking on with curious or suspicious eyes. Dorav and Steva paced just outside the ring of guards, which eased Joseph's mind, if only a little. The going was slower now that the guards surrounded them and the traffic was greater, and nearly another hour passed before the tunnel rounded a final corner and opened into a massive cavern. Joseph was speechless as the dwarven city spread open before him. Kaillë gasped. "By all the winds and stars," she whispered, her hands covering her mouth, "it's *beautiful*."

The main cavern of the city stretched a hundred feet below them, stone towers and crystal spires thrusting up from the floor to their level, and some another fifty feet above that. Crystal walkways spanned between many of the towers, and strange torches, glowing fungus, and shining glass bathed the chamber in a sea of scintillating light and shadow in hues and intensities not unlike a sunset. All along the nearer walls, walkways allowed access to the open archways of apartments and stores, tier after tier stretching fifty feet above their heads and down to the cavern floor below. Joseph supposed the farther walls were the same, but the sight of them was lost to the distance. To his right, a series of waterfalls ran into a system of troughs and canals that delivered the water quietly to pools scattered throughout the districts he could see from his vantage, all lit in flitting color by some kind of luminous creatures. Throughout this tableau the city was in motion, guards and civilians hurrying from place to place along the ground and tiers, dwarves in regal robes striding across the walkways, and pairs of giant badgers pulling carts, some full of crates or sacks, others piled high with raw ore.

Delia, Joseph thought, *what I wouldn't give to share this sight with you*. Kaillë moved closer to him, one hand still held to her face in disbelief, and he resisted the urge to shift away, fighting down the guilt of enjoying her nearness, her unabashed wonder at the hidden world spread out before them.

The guards, charitably, had halted at the vista, letting the visitors absorb the sight. Dorav turned to face them, his hand scratching Steva absently between the ears. "Welcome to Tra'id-Stie'che, the Streets of Twilight. Rover that I am, the return to her always warms the heart, don't it?"

The party nodded dumbly as the guards began moving again. After walking to the left around the terrace, the group turned right down the nearest flying walkway which, like its neighbors at this elevation, was broad and formed of smooth stone with heavy railings on either side. "I was glad when I came down here I wasn't scared of tight spaces," Rook muttered, "I never dreamed I'd have to be glad I wasn't scared of *heights*." It was true, Joseph realized as he glanced over the right-hand railing; there was nothing beneath him but air for the hundred feet to the cavern floor.

After only fifty feet the walkway entered an archway into an ornately carved tower, its surface a masterpiece of bas relief behind statuary of stalwart dwarves on ledges at every level. The next half hour was an endless stream of hallways, stairs, and guards trading orders in the Dwarven tongue. Dorav and Steva stayed with them during the whole walk, and no dwarf so much as raised an eye at the giant badger's presence, nor Stitch's either for that matter, though it was becoming clear they were walking the halls of the Ninth Clan's seat of government.

Finally the party was led to chambers where they could

refresh themselves before their audience with the elders. Joseph had to crouch to clear the doorway, and even once past it he felt the ceiling brush his hair if he stood up straight, but the room was otherwise appointed well. Ewers of clean, cold water and basins were provided for washing, followed by small bottles of lightly colored powders that gave off a variety of pleasing fragrances. Joseph avoided masking scents of any kind as a rule, but he had no idea of the dwarven customs around such things, and he had to admit bathing hadn't been his priority over the last few days. He selected a muskier scent and tapped a bit over his clothing before dressing again.

The guards had indicated they would return for them when the elders were ready, so Joseph reclined on the short mattress and tried to stretch the weariness from his muscles. The edge of the mattress came just to his knees, so he rested his heels on the stone floor and closed his eyes, taking advantage of a rare opportunity to rest in relative safety. Not that he trusted the dwarves completely, but if they were his enemies, he had no hope of escape, and any other enemies had as little hope of getting to him without their consent, so he surrendered to the overwhelming inevitability of his situation and began to doze.

He had no idea how much time had passed when he opened his eyes to the sound of Dorav clearing his throat from the doorway. Joseph rose, stretched his back, and looked down at the dwarf. "I've made my report," Dorav said, "and the elders are ready to speak with you."

"What did you think of their attitude?" Joseph asked.

"I'm no expert on *them*. I've only spoken to them once before, and if I have my way I never will again."

Joseph grimaced. "Are they really that bad?"

"I'm a rover. If I liked being that close to the dwarves in charge, I'd live in the city like a normal person. Listen, a dwarf elder is nothing if not just, but life don't work down here if everybody ain't hewing the same tunnel, and sometimes things get strict. However things go, tell the truth. The elders can hear the lie in a man's voice like you hear me talking now."

"I've never wasted time speaking false, Dorav."

"It was just advice, surface-walker, I didn't mean nothin' by it. Depending on the elders' word, we may not walk the same stretch again, but I've found nothin' ill in ye, Joseph. Best of luck in whatever brings you down here." He extended his hand, and Joseph clasped it.

Chapter Ten

Minutes later the party stood in a spacious gallery lit in even, yellow light by some glowing substance that hung from the ceiling in glass orbs. Two arcing terraces rose before them, each only two feet high, on which sat the assembled dwarven elders on simple seats of stone. There were about twenty in all, though Joseph did not undertake an exact count as he fought down the anxiety of appearing before such a crowd of government officials. About half wore uniforms similar to the guards that had escorted them to the tower and the others that now stood around the room, so Joseph assumed they represented the military. He could not guess at the background of the rest.

Rook and the elves, being of smaller stature, had been provided with dwarven clothes; they were short and wide, but the group made due. Kaillë wore a simple, gray tunic she had managed to gather and belt so its folds appeared more voluminous than simply baggy, and she had plaited her hair into a long braid and coiled its length on top of her head, detracting nothing from the regal bearing of her shoulders as she stood before the dwarven leaders. Joseph

Identity & Community 115

had been surprised none of them had been asked to surrender their weapons, not that he was under any illusion of what use they would be against the long pikes and superior coordination of the dwarven guards. Still, he wore his knife openly, and his quiver and bow on his back gave him some comfort, even though he had unstrung the weapon. Kaillë had the naked short sword he had given her tucked through her belt, and though he knew she couldn't use it, he had to admit she wore it well.

After a full minute of simply watching them stand, one of the dwarven elders spoke. "Why are you here?" he demanded.

Kaillë did not hesitate. "We entered your realm on urgent business. We were glad to find Dorav the Rover, as we had no wish to cause offense by wandering your lands without permission or escort. I will answer your question directly, but first I must point out that, to the best of my knowledge, this is the first meeting between our peoples. I am Kaillë Windsong, Chieftain of the Windrider Clan. Your city is magnificent, and we are honored to be your guests."

Another dwarf spoke up. "Your kind words are appreciated, Chieftain. I am called Vodeen. We do not know the annals of the other clans, but you are correct that the Ninth Clan has never hosted elves before. We have discussed the matter and can see little benefit to friendship with your people, but we hope that we can continue to be peaceful neighbors, and perhaps, in time, less aloof to one another. Much of that future, however, will depend upon your answer to my colleague's question. You should give it now."

"We came seeking the Hoard of Dalviir," Kaillë answered.

"We have no knowledge of this hoard or interest in it," the first dwarf answered, "but if it is in our lands it is ours by right, and you may not have it. Your business with us is concluded. You will be returned to the surface under oath never to speak of this place to anyone. Your companions will be kept here under pain of death to assure your silence. Guards, escort them from our presence."

The guards began to move, but Kaillë stepped forward and halted them with a look at the nearest one. "I know very little of your people," Kaillë said. "I see much that I admire, but I hear only rash decisions. You see no value in friendship without meeting me in person, you deny my right to a thing without knowing what it is, you demand to keep it without knowing whether you want it, and you hold my companions lives over my head without knowing what pains I might endure to rescue them. Surely the wonders of your city were not built on a foundation of this kind of thinking."

Vodeen chuckled. "Her tongue is quicker than yours, Zozak, and only the less blunt for being sharper, I think. You speak truth, Chieftain, our stance on surface-walkers is harsh, perhaps to rashness. At most times it has needed to be. You speak well, however, and more patiently than we have. That said, if you come beneath the earth looking for things you *do* have any rightful claim to, it would be the first time any surface-walker had done so in this clan. Tell us, what is this hoard you seek?"

"I take it, then, that you do not know the name of Dalviir, Scourge of the Fourth Dynasty?" Kaillë asked.

"That is a human name, called by the eras that humans use to reckon time. We have no interest in human history," a different dwarf replied.

"You may have need to very soon," Kaillë answered. "Rook, you have studied the Fourth Dynasty and the Hoard more than anyone. Explain it to the dwarves, please."

Rook gulped as she stepped forward in her ill-fitting brown robes. "The Fourth Dynasty ended centuries ago on the surface," she began, "with the death of the Sorcerer

King Dalviir." Her last two words were drowned by the sounds of laughter, grunts, and shouts.

"Sorcerer!" boomed the dwarf called Zozak. "Magic? We give you the privilege of time to explain your purposes and you waste our time with talk of nonsense and foolishness. Spare us your surface superstitions."

Joseph could not stay silent. "I am no superstitious fool," he shouted back, "but only a *blind* fool denies what he has seen with his eyes. I lost nearly all of my men in two heartbeats to a sorcerer armed with the power of Dalviir, and there wasn't enough left of them to *bury*. When you scoff that power you mock that tragedy, and I will not leave that unanswered." Joseph's hand was on his knife.

"Warriors, warriors," Vodeen said, standing, "calmer heads, please. Chieftain," he continued to Kaillë, "we meant no offense. It has been our experience, however, that surface-walkers cite magic as the reason for anything they don't understand. They see a dwarven lightstick, for instance, and call it 'magic', never imagining that we learned the secrets of the luminous creatures and fungi in our midst and found ways to reproduce their light. In the beauty of our crystal walkways they see 'magic', not generations of gemcraft and hard work. To us, these are very strange beliefs, and we have yet to see anything of the surface world that cannot be explained by reason."

Kaillë moved closer to Joseph. "I wasn't prepared for this," she whispered.

Joseph shrugged, wishing he could help but having nothing to offer.

Kaillë nodded, then turned, resolute, to face the dwarven elders. "We will have to table discussion of the Hoard's power for another time," Kaillë said, "because the fact is that others are pursuing the prize as well. They may be in your tunnels already, and unlike us they will not come with peaceful intentions. These are some of the same men that, only days ago, razed my village and slaughtered more than half of my people."

The elders bowed their heads for a moment, then one looked up and spoke. "You have our deepest sorrow for the lifeblood of your people. We did not understand your situation. We will dispatch guards to the tunnels immediately; do you need to suspend our discussions until your period of mourning has passed?"

"I will mourn in my own way, as time allows," Kaillë replied. "We must know more of the Hoard, though. The invaders may get past your guards, or others may come, even years from now. Deny its power if you will, but others will not. It is in your own best interest to destroy the Hoard, and to let us spread the word that you have. It is the only way to curtail constant incursions into your realm."

Murmurs passed through the body of elders, then one spoke. "This is a very bold request, Chieftain. We will have to confer upon it. First we must, finally, discover just what is this 'hoard' that you are talking about. You may dispense with its history; only tell us how we may know what it is and where we might have stored it, assuming that we do have it."

Kaillë looked to Joseph, so he spoke. "The chamber where the Hoard would have been found is near the surface, not far from where Dorav found us. It is a vault of unnatural, black stone that had been tunneled into from below with precise stonework, such as I have only seen made by dwarves. I do not know how long ago. According to Dorav, the region was lost to trolls two generations ago. Does that help?"

"Ah," remembered a wizened dwarf who had not yet spoken, "the young human must mean the Glowstones." Several of the older dwarves nodded assent. "You see, in my father's time, there was an expedition into the region you describe. They discovered a mysterious chamber of black stone; inside it was a collection of twelve small orbs that glowed with light from within – sometimes more, sometimes less, but always glowing. I served on a team that studied them for a time, but we never learned the secrets of their light..."

"No surprises there," Rook muttered.

"...so we placed them in a vault to await a time when our knowledge was a match for their creator's. We certainly cannot destroy such treasures."

"You *must* destroy such treasures," Joseph insisted. "You don't understand their power. They don't just glow; in the wrong hands they're the most lethal things I've ever seen. If you deny magic, call it by whatever name you will; if you trust reason, then hear the words of a witness. I'm told you can tell when people are lying to you, so you can see *I* believe what I'm saying. So am I mad, or am I right?"

A ripple of surprise ran up and down the two rows of seated elders. At last one spoke. "We have heard your words. We will now confer on the merits of your arguments and make our decision."

The elders rose and adjourned to a table at the back of the hall, leaving Joseph and his companions to stand and wait. Rook's eyes were stormy, and her mouth was turned down in a scowl. "You've fixed me up right good, haven't you, hunter? Now the dwarves will either never let us within a hundred feet of the Hoard, or they'll destroy it themselves without ever letting us see it. You can't *do* that to me, Joseph, we had a deal. First pick, remember, you *promised* me that!"

Rook's voice had risen, and some of the elders looked over at Joseph's group. Kaillë silenced the louder human with a look. "Enough, Rook. It's time, past time, that you told your secret. Those dwarves are threatening to keep all of you here, and who knows what Turov and Aglar might do if they get past the dwarven guards. Lives are in the balance here, so let's hear your interest in all this. The truth, for once."

Rook looked down, her jaw bunched and face red, and when she looked back up again, Joseph was shocked to see tears in her eyes. "It's my brother," she finally whispered. "Our parents died when we were small, and he took care of me. Then the war took him away. It gave him back, but it gave him back broken. He got an axe in the back, and now his legs don't work. The healers managed to keep him alive, but they couldn't fix the damage. He..." Rook stopped for a moment, her lower lip quivering, but then she swallowed hard, sniffed, blinked out a few tears that she wiped away roughly with the heel of her hand, and continued. "He was an acrobat. He'd work with a troupe sometimes, or just toss out a hat on the street and work his best stunts. He was the best; even in the lean times, he could always impress the crowds enough to keep our bellies full and our backs warm. Now... He taught me what he knew; I can take care of what he needs, but...he loved the shows. He just wastes away now, moaning about the war, hating life. I couldn't bear it any longer. The legends say that some of Dalviir's work wasn't just about taking life; some was about giving it back. He never got any farther with true immortality than any other mad wizard, but if even half of the other stories of his miracles are true, then something in that Hoard will let my brother walk again."

"That's why you were quick to let us find a wizard to verify your choice," Kaillë realized. "You'd have needed one anyway to find the right artifact and thought you could get us to foot the bill."

Rook shrugged with a sheepish smile. "First rule of the scam: Get the mark to think what you need is really what they need."

"You could have just asked," Joseph said. "It's a worthy enough cause, and you've been of use."

"And you'd have just taken my word for it all and brought me along," Rook replied, her tone sarcastic. "Don't think I'm dumb just 'cause I'm young and pretty, hunter. Anyway, now you know, so back to the matter at hand. It's all well and good for the world if the dwarves agree to destroy the stones, but that doesn't do a lick of good for my brother, now, does it?"

"Well," Joseph replied, "the good news is that if they don't agree to destroy them, they may not be too difficult to convince to let you have one, since they don't believe they're worth what they're worth, anyway."

After a few more minutes of waiting, an elder addressed the group. "We believe your words are the truth, as you see it, but we will not destroy our own property on the word of strangers. If possessing these items brings us danger from the outside, then that is our affair, not yours. We acknowledge some danger if the stones were to fall out of our possession, so we agree to show you to the vault where the stones are kept to assure you that they are safely locked away. You may speak to us once more after you have seen the vault, at which time your ultimate fate will be determined."

Joseph recognized the pattern of snap judgment, pause for rebuttal, and final judgment from his first dwarven encounter during the war and knew further argument was useless. One of the elders in military dress moved down from the tiers and approached the company, motioning to two guards to fall in behind him as he walked. "I am called Zev," he said to Kaillë. "I have been appointed to show you to the vault. You will see that it is quite secure. Please, follow me."

They followed the dwarf out of the audience chamber into a hallway and turned to the right. At the end of the hall was what appeared to be a small, empty closet, only a little larger than necessary to accommodate their group. A single dwarf stood inside near a panel of levers. Their chaperone, Zev, waited outside next to a metal tube protruding from the wall. He spoke into it in his own tongue, and after a moment, a reply came back. Afterward he joined them in the closet and closed a heavy door. The dwarf operating the levers pulled one of them, and a slight tremor ran through the room. He slowly pushed another lever, and the whole room started moving downward. Joseph was startled for a moment, but as the room slowly took on speed, the two dwarves remained calm, so he took a deep breath and kept his head. "You have many wonders here," he said to Zev. "I have known tree-dwellers who use lifts and pulleys to move things up from the ground, and I was in a palace once, briefly, that used something like this to take food from floor to floor, but I've never heard of it being done on this scale, or of anyone trusting it enough to carry passengers."

"We have harnessed the power of falling water and of springs," the dwarf replied, "and we use physical labor, both dwarf and badger, when there is need, amplified by counterweights and gears and other machines. Our scholars have great hope for steam as a medium of transforming the power of fire into a power of motion. Their early experiments have been quite successful, but it will require more time to expand to a practical application."

"You seem very knowledgeable about these things for a military man," Joseph stated.

Zev smiled, a subtle expression to be sure, but noticeable. "I suppose that's true. A dwarf with open ears and mind can learn much from the company of the council of elders, but I have to admit that some of my brothers in the guard are not so fascinated by such discoveries as others."

At length the falling room came to a gentle stop, and the door was opened from the outside by a dwarven guard. A half-dozen others stood on either side of the adjoining hallway, and Zev led Joseph's party out into their midst, then gave an order in dwarven that caused them to fall into formation around the elves and humans. They walked down the hallway to an outside door and exited the tower at street level into a dense but orderly crowd of foot and cart traffic. An open-topped carriage of metal stood before them, and the elder invited the group to climb aboard. Joseph stowed his bow under one of the bench seats and was grateful the dwarf-sized vehicle wasn't enclosed; as it was his knees were sharply bent as he sat on the farthest end of the front bench. He noticed then none of the carriages passing on the street had roofs either and realized in a world without rain or snow or significant changes in temperature, such enclosures had likely never occurred to the dwarven people. The rest of the party stepped onto the carriage, followed by Zev, and at last they had all settled in across the three bench seats. Though the legroom was noticeably cramped even for the shorter members of the group, there was ample space at either side, the dwarves being far broader than the lithe elves. Kaillë had followed Joseph and sat next to him while Stitch laid down at his feet. As soon as everyone was aboard, the dwarven guards jumped onto rails on the outside of the vehicle, the driver gave a shout, and the quartet of badgers pulling the coach set off at a brisk trot.

Chapter Eleven

𝕱or several minutes they rode, taking in the exotic bustle of the dwarven world as they traveled away from the heart of the city into darker, more remote tunnels. They saw fewer and fewer dwarves as they went, save for the guards at a series of checkpoints where they were obliged to stop while the drivers presented documents to the guard captains. "I'm surprised the vault is so far from the main districts of the city," Rook commented.

"We may not label what we do not understand out of superstition or fear," Zev commented, "but we offer it due respect. It would be foolish to store things that may yet pose a danger to us in a populated area."

At last the coach stopped, and the guards opened the door in the carriage's short sidewall so the party could exit. Before them was what appeared to be a blank stone wall. "This is the vault," the elder declared.

"Of course it is," Joseph answered, his tone wry.

"I'm quite serious," Zev said.

"Oh, I know," Joseph chuckled. "I'm just...I've had experience with your doors once before."

"Ah," the dwarf replied. "In any case, if I might trouble you to look to the floor for a moment..."

As the group complied, they heard the elder step away to an area on the side wall, then a subtle rasp of stones rubbing together. When they raised their heads, a huge pair of locks was before them where before there had been only rock.

"Behind these two locks is another, master lock that opens the vault doors," Zev explained. "The doors themselves are two feet of stone and steel layers, and if the locks are destroyed they will jam the doors shut permanently. As you can see, these stones you seek are quite safe from any outside invader."

"Unless they use magic," Kaillë muttered to Joseph in Elven.

"What was that?" the elder asked.

"Oh, nothing," Kaillë answered.

"So," Zev resumed, "what other demonstrations might I..."

A sudden drumbeat echoed up from the tunnel, followed by a series of horn blasts.

"We have to go," the elder ordered. "Please get back into the carriage immediately."

Sensing the urgency in the dwarf's voice, Joseph ushered the party to comply, but he asked "What's going on?" as he stood by the cart waiting for the rest of his company to climb aboard.

"The city has come under attack," the elder answered.

"Is it the men we told you about?" Joseph asked. "Did they get past the guards you sent?"

"I don't know where they may be," Zev said as he climbed in after Joseph. "The signal drums indicate something more serious. It seems a horde of trolls has broken into one of the main tunnels from below and launched an attack at the lower gates."

"Are we in danger here?"

"Not directly, but the guard has gone on high alert and is being redeployed to attend the threat even as we speak. We cannot guarantee your safety so far from the heart of the city. We will take you back to the tower of the elders; there is nowhere more secure."

The badgers had started off at a furious pace, and without stopping for the checkpoints, Joseph knew they would not have long before they were back at the relative safety of the tower. His senses were on edge, but he reminded himself there was nothing he could do in the coach and tried to steady his nerves. Still, he pulled his bow from under the seats and strung it, fighting against the cramped quarters of the carriage as he did. He looked to Kaillë to gauge her reaction to the danger and followed her gaze to Rook. The human girl's eyes were wide with fear and hopelessness, and she bit her lower lip so hard Joseph feared she would draw blood. He knew the dwarves were people of honor, if perhaps a staid, rigid version of it at times, and were unlikely to ignore a selfless action on their behalf. "Elder," he said, "when we return to the tower, I would have the rest of my people kept safe, but I intend to join the battle if I may."

The elder looked keenly into Joseph's eyes before speaking. "Very well. I will attach you to a unit of Irregulars when we return to the tower. Thank you."

Joseph nodded. Kaillë, sitting next to him, leaned close and spoke in Elven, keeping her speech simple so Joseph could translate it as she did. "It will be dangerous, Joseph."

"Are you trying to dissuade me?"

"No. I've learned not to. Only be careful. If I'm to lose you, I would want it to be by choice, not by death."

"I'll come back," Joseph answered. Kaillë did not speak again, but she didn't lean away, and Joseph didn't force her to.

Identity & Community 127

The coach thundered on, and in another minute they were back in the city's main cavern, forced to slow to avoid the heavy traffic of civilian dwarves moving to safety and soldiers heading toward the battle. They were still a quarter-mile away from the tower when they reached an intersection completely blocked by a column of warriors jogging through. "We should proceed on foot," Zev said. "I could order the column to stop to let us pass, but I choose not to."

"Don't hamper the fighting men," Joseph agreed, "we can walk the rest of the way."

They filed out of the coach, and the guards formed up around Joseph's party and ran them across the street one at a time in the short breaks between squads. As he awaited his turn, Joseph heard a familiar voice. "Joseph," Dorav called, "what are you and your lot still doing here? Bad time to be about town."

Dorav and Steva walked in the midst of a small company of dwarves, all heavily armed with axes and spears, but not in uniform. Joseph looked down at the elder. "Would these be one of those units of Irregulars you mentioned?"

The elder nodded. "Go with them, if it is still your wish."

The thought of battle quickened his pulse and sent his gut into knots. *My wish? My intention, anyway.*

After handing Stitch's lead off to Zev, which the elder accepted with a look of surprise, Joseph took a deep breath and approached Dorav. "Thought I'd stay around awhile and show you rovers a thing or two," he finally answered the ax-toting dwarf. "Show me where I can do the most good."

"Stick close to me and Steva," Dorav told him, his face serious.

As Joseph fell in with the group, he turned a last look toward where the elves had crossed the busy street. He saw

Kaillë looking over her shoulder at him, but then her face was lost in the crowd.

~ * ~

A few minutes later, Joseph found himself manning a makeshift barricade behind one of the less-used entrances to the city, a simple gate of iron in a dimly-lit stretch of plain tunnel.

"This was a main thoroughfare a few generations back," Dorav explained, "but when our ancestors decided they needed a larger main access, they couldn't expand this one without risking a cave-in, so they had to build somewhere else, and this tunnel became less popular. It still gets enough traffic from a couple key points, though, so we can't fill it in. When trouble hits, it falls to us free-roaming types to hold the gate, and others like it."

"Do the trolls usually try these smaller tunnels?" Joseph asked, eyes intent on the darkness ahead.

"Trolls are trolls," Dorav replied, "primitive and unpredictable. No way we can suss out their battle plan when they don't have one themselves."

Joseph saw nothing but shadow, but one of the dwarves must have sensed movement. "Who goes there?" he shouted.

There was no answer but a gang of shapes bursting out of the darkness, hideous creatures the like of which Joseph had never seen. They stood a head taller than the dwarves, but no less broad, so while Joseph compared them to a short but particularly stocky human, to the dwarves their size must have been intimidating. They also had the usual number and configuration of arms and legs, but after that any similarity to human or dwarf was void. Their arms, legs, and backs were covered thickly with coarse, black hair that built to bushy manes around their hairless faces. The exposed skin on their faces and fronts was hard and pebbly and no lighter than their coats. Their faces were hideous, eyeless visions of savagery, huge ears and upturned noses like those of a bat, and mouths filled with rows of sharp, bony ridges in place of teeth. They wore no armor and carried only the simplest weapons or none at all, but they threw themselves at the gate without apparent thought or fear, tearing at the locks with their bare, clawed hands. Their strength must have been great for, much to Joseph's dread, the bars bent under their initial assault.

Joseph loosed his bow at the troll directly before him, but the arrow sunk into its chest no deeper than the arrowhead itself, and if the target noticed the wound at all, it seemed to make him more angry than afraid. Joseph drew and shot again, and this time the beast let out a hellish shriek and fell back with an arrow protruding from the place where its eye should have been. Joseph was sharply aware, however, that he had only half a dozen arrows left in his quiver, and he did not relish the thought of going hand-to-hand with a pack of ferocious trolls. A quiet part of him that valued survival over duty wanted to quit the field and return to the tower to tell Rook to get her own damn healing artifact, but the greater part of him knew there could be no recanting his decision to join this fight now that men were counting on him, and deep down he knew gaining a bargaining advantage with the dwarves had not been his only motivation. He still owed a debt to dwarves for helping his men, and years and distance had not diminished it.

Somewhere between Joseph's first and second shots, the dwarves on either side of him launched a volley of crossbow bolts, but Joseph, his hands moving like lightning, had emptied his quiver before the crossbows had a chance to reload. For a moment the enemy fell back in shock under the swift and accurate attacks, and had he been able to sustain it Joseph believed he might have convinced the mob to go spend their lives someplace else, but when he stopped shooting they redoubled their efforts, trampling bodies or dragging them out of the way to get to the gates.

"Try that," Dorav shouted over the snarling of the trolls and handed Joseph his cocked-and-loaded crossbow. "Just aim dead center."

Joseph did as he was told and found, indeed, the crossbow had power enough to plunge through the troll's tough, thick hide and bring the enemy down. Truly it was a formidable weapon, and better-designed than human crossbows he had tried, but for all its power, it was simply too slow. *If only we had twice as many* was his last thought before the lock gave way and the gates burst open. One more salvo and the trolls were upon them.

It was tooth and claw against ax and spear at the top of the barricade, with everything the trolls lacked in armament or strategy made up in numbers and sheer viciousness. Joseph had taken a spear from behind the barricade and thrust unceasingly downward, trying to keep the enemy from gaining a foothold, but there were simply too many. When there was no more room to climb up, other trolls started tearing at the barricade itself, smashing crates into splinters or tearing broken cart pieces clear of the wall.

Suddenly a troll bounded up before Joseph, and he braced his feet and thrust his spear upward into the warty chest. The troll went limp, but then the spear snapped under the impact, and Joseph lost his balance, landing on his shoulder blades on the hard stone behind the barricade's short step.

He reeled for a moment as he tried to gather his legs under him to stand, then heard a voice cry out in dwarven, using a tone more like an order than a battle cry. Joseph didn't understand the command but followed the nearest dwarf in a sideways retreat to press his back against the right-hand wall of the tunnel. A moment later the barricade burst apart and trolls started streaming through. Joseph readied his knife before him, but before any trolls could draw near, a chorus of low, rumbling growls sounded through the tunnels as half a dozen giant badgers charged forward. Joseph knew the aggression and strength of their small, surface-dwelling cousins, but the ferocity of these creatures beggared description. They bowled over the enemy like ninepins, digging their claws in as they trampled them down.

Not five feet in front of Joseph a troll bellowed a challenge and charged a badger head-on, only for the badger to open his mouth, thrust forward his lean, muscular jaws, and snap the creature's arm and shoulder clean off. In only moments the trolls were mobbing the badgers, ten or a dozen to each animal, and the dwarves had leapt to again, either striking at the trolls where they were or dragging them off the animals to finish them on the stone floor. Joseph did his part, using his superior height and leverage to help hurl trolls to the floor before they could do too much damage to the badgers, his knife flashing into atrophied eye sockets or across throats. The badgers, for their part, hadn't ceased dealing out carnage as they turned to one another to savage any trolls their partners couldn't reach.

The strategy was brutal and effective, but it came with a high cost. In minutes all the trolls had died or fled back into the deeper tunnels, but five dwarves and three badgers lay bleeding and moaning on the ground, and it was certain some would not survive. Joseph saw movement and realized two more dwarves were among the wounded, shoving their way out from under the wreckage of barricade pieces and dead trolls that littered the ground. A moment later Joseph heard weeping, and when he looked toward the sound he realized one of the injured badgers was

Steva; Dorav knelt over him, petting him between the ears as he wept. It was the first time Joseph had seen deep emotion in a dwarf, and he felt an immediate kinship for the closest thing he had to a friend among this strange and distant race. The thing that had always troubled him most about elves was their stoicism during painful times, and it was somehow comforting, if bitterly, bitterly so, to see this proud rover displaying such unabashed grief for his fallen friend. Joseph walked over to the dwarf, cleaning the thick, black troll blood from his knife, and knelt next to Dorav as Steva whimpered and licked at his hand like a frightened dog.

Joseph's heart was broken for the loyal animal, but first he looked up to the twisted gates and shattered barricade. "Will they come again? We can't hope to hold again without reinforcements."

As if in answer, a series of horn blasts echoed through the tunnels. "The main surge at the gate has been turned back," one of the dwarves explained. "The guard has put the enemy to flight and will likely give chase to discourage another attack. We should be safe."

Joseph saw others were already tending to the wounded dwarves, so hoping against hope, he knelt down next to Steva and tried to assess the damage. His hurts were many, and Joseph had no doubt he was in great pain, but only one wound was deep, and Joseph didn't think it an empty or cruel hope to say, "I make no promise, Dorav, but I do not lie when I say I have saved creatures from greater harm than this. If we can only get him loaded into a cart and back to the city..."

"No," Dorav, argued, "you don't understand. Wounds from trolls are riddled with contagion. Dwarves have long been immune, but our badgers are not so lucky."

"Give up if you will," Joseph said, petting Steva's muzzle, "but I won't. There are wonders in your world, but there are wonders in mine, too. The world of the sun and growing things is not without its medicines, maybe greater than yours. We have some in our supplies, so sit and weep if you want to, but I'm going to find a cart and a pair of healthy badgers to pull it."

Joseph was less than halfway to the city when a team of dwarves driving carts stopped him in the tunnel. "What are you doing here, surface-walker?" their leader demanded.

"Trying to find help for our wounded; I was just fighting with a rover unit."

"How many wounded do you have?" the dwarf asked, keeping attention strictly to the urgent matters at hand.

"Seven dwarves, three badgers."

"Nothing to be done for the beasts," the dwarf said, motioning one of the carts forward as he prepared to turn the rest around.

"I have medicines that may work, if we hurry. Will you help, or do I need to move on?"

The dwarf paused, then motioned for three more carts to follow Joseph, who led them to the aftermath of the skirmish as quickly as he could.

Chapter Twelve

It took every able dwarf working together to get the three badgers loaded into carts, a task which was forced to wait until the wounded dwarves had been rushed back toward the city. Of the seven, one had already succumbed to blood loss, and another was given only faint hope, but the rest were expected to recover fully. Joseph raced back ahead of the wounded badgers and found his way to the elders' tower. Once inside, a guard escorted him to the chambers where his people were staying. He searched his pack for the herbs and extracts he would need, drawing on the knowledge of healing plants he had learned from his wife years before, and began making poultices on the spot. The cart drivers, by his instruction, came directly to the base of the tower, where Joseph and the elves, now back in their own clothing, began treating the badgers as soon as they arrived. Only minutes later, the work was done, and there was nothing more to do but wait.

As Stitch wandered over to him, his rope lead trailing, at last Joseph took stock, checking that each member of his little band was present and unhurt. A dagger of icy dread pierced his gut as he made his count. "Where is Rook?" he asked, his voice thick with suspicion.

"There were great throngs coming and going from the tower after you left us, and...somehow we got separated," Kaillë explained.

"You lost her *again*?" Joseph demanded.

"She must be somewhere close by," Tes'oriv said. "Where else would she go?"

Joseph raised an eyebrow at Tes'oriv, then shifted his look to Kaillë.

"The vault," the young chieftain realized. "Should we go after her?"

"We don't have much choice," Joseph replied. "We may have gained enough respect with the dwarves to convince them to give her what she needs, but if she does something stupid first, there's no telling how severe the penalty will be."

The party was still under guard, and Joseph looked at the young dwarves who had been left to tend them while the rest were called up to the battle. He whispered to Kaillë. "One or two of us could probably slip away, but I don't want to split up, or become fugitives, for that matter. Can you get them to let us go?"

Kaillë considered for a moment. "From what I've seen of dwarven discipline, I doubt it. I might be able to convince them to escort us there."

"I'd rather they weren't around to see it if Rook is trying to crack that vault, but if that's our opening, we'd best take it, or it'll be too late."

Kaillë squared her shoulders and addressed the nearest guard. "Now that the battle is over, we need to conclude our business here. The elders had granted us permission to make an inspection of your vault, and we were interrupted. We need to return, and quickly."

The half-dozen dwarven guards looked at one another,

and Joseph could imagine they were trading thoughts, not yet as forged into one mind as the older unit he had encountered during the war. At last one of the guards spoke. "We will escort you as far as the first checkpoint. It will be up to the dhor-zabh there whether your prior papers of passage are still in force or if new ones will be required." With that, the guards formed up around them and started down the street at a trot.

"Hey," came a shout from behind them, "where are you off to?"

Joseph tensed for a moment, but then realized the voice was Dorav's. "We need to go back to the vault," Joseph called over his shoulder.

Dorav sprinted to catch up with them. "I'll come with you, if it's alright. Steva is sleeping now. Even if he doesn't pull through, I'm in your debt for giving him a fighting chance."

"Glad to have you along," Joseph said. "I'm not sure what we'll find when we get there."

~ * ~

What they found, after several minutes of jogging through darker and darker tunnels, was carnage. The barrier at the first checkpoint had been destroyed, and the floor was littered with dead dwarven guards and a single civilian whose throat had been cut.

"How did the trolls get all the way out here?" Dorav wondered, his voice raw.

"They didn't," Joseph answered, inspecting the nearest body. "These wounds were made with sharp blades, not claws and teeth, and here..." He crossed over to another corpse and pulled an arrow from its neck. "Aglar's men."

The guards were agitated, and became more so when Joseph wiped the arrow on his cloak and returned it to his

Identity & Community 137

empty quiver. "I'm sorry," he said flatly, "I need the arrow. We need to move quickly."

"We will remain here," one of the guards proclaimed. "One of us will go back for reinforcements; no one will advance until they arrive."

"Do what you want," Joseph replied as he took Stitch out of his harness. "I'm not waiting for anything. If the Baron manages to get to those stones, we're all as good as dead. I'm not going to stand around here while that happens, assuming it hasn't happened already." Then he was off and running, not worrying who would choose to follow.

He stopped to think when he reached the second checkpoint. It was clear the humans had not taken the dwarven guards completely by surprise in this second battle; there were signs of a brief skirmish, and two of the Baron's fighters lay dead on the stone of the tunnel. No arrows were in evidence, leading Joseph to believe the dwarves had rushed out to give battle before Aglar's scouts had time to line up clean shots. Joseph knew there were three more checkpoints ahead, but no sounds of battle echoed back to him, and the blood on the floor was thick and sticky. He remembered no side tunnels leaving this course on their first trip to the vault, so either the enemy was still confounded by the vault door, which Joseph considered unlikely since no enemy sentries had been sent back up the tunnel to guard the approach, or they'd made it back to the main tunnel before the band had even reached it, meaning by now they could be anywhere. "We may be too late," Joseph muttered to the group that jogged up from behind. Dorav had accompanied all the elves, including Kaillë, and Joseph mentally cursed himself for not remembering to insist she stay behind with the guards.

Again they were on the move, Joseph keeping a tally of dead humans as he went. The numbers grew at each guard station, but he reckoned the enemy still had at least thirty men to throw at him.

At last they came to the vault, and Joseph's worst fears were realized when he saw its great stone and steel doors standing wide open. No damage was evident, and Joseph found it unlikely Turov or Aglar could even have found the vault alone…so there could now be no doubt that Rook was every bit as good as she'd claimed to be. Joseph was the first to step into the vault, a smaller space than he'd expected after the grandeur of the main dwarven cavern. Inside the oblong space, perhaps thirty feet long and half that across, were shelves of tools, weapons, gems, and artifacts Joseph had no name for, but his eyes were drawn to a smashed crate on the floor to his left. Just feet away was a pile of charred bone and ash containing a few blackened steel rings and buckles and a sooty two-handed sword. "Looks like Aglar waited too long to make his play," he said to the group. He turned to Dorav. "I guess your people aren't the only ones who underestimated these stones."

Dorav just shook his head, his eyes uncomprehending.

"Now we have a real problem," Joseph said. "The Baron will be drawn to the nearest concentration of magical power. I can't say how much he knows of magic, but we have to assume the worst: that he's studied the rituals he needs to attune the stones. When I was up against this threat during the war, a local villager was able to point the way, but down here the locals don't even believe magic *exists*, much less where to go to find it."

"Joseph," Dorav said from behind him, "what does this mean?"

Joseph turned and saw Dorav standing from where he had knelt by the shattered crate, lifting a small, dark object in his hand. It was a black feather, tied with beadwork.

Joseph smiled. "It means Rook is still alive, or was…and she wants us to follow her." He took the feather and held it out to Stitch. "Here you go, Stitch, get the scent. Now find Rook, boy. Go find Rook."

Stitch wandered the vault for a moment, sniffing everything, then seemed to hit on something familiar and trotted out the large doors. He moved past the nearest checkpoint without slowing, then another twenty yards before making a hard left and stopping at the wall. He followed the wall a few feet in each direction, sniffing at the base, then returned to the original spot and began scratching at the stone.

"There's a door here," Joseph realized. "Dorav, can you get it open?"

"I can try," the dwarf answered. He stood over Stitch for a moment, talking to himself. "Let's see, this is an older tunnel, built in the fourth or fifth decade after the city founding, I believe, so based on the standards at the time, the switch should be right about...here." He moved a couple paces to the right and placed his hand on the wall. Nothing happened. He scratched his head.

"Are you sure that's the place?" Kaillë asked.

"Positive," the dwarf replied.

"This isn't good," Joseph said. "Rook clearly went this way, but the Baron must have found some way to jam the mechanism from the other side. We'll have to find another way. Dorav, do you..."

"Wait," the dwarf said, holding up a hand for silence. Suddenly he nodded. "There." He moved his hand down six inches and pressed again, and this time only a moment passed before a door whispered open, sending Stitch dodging backward at the sudden movement. "Sorry," Dorav shrugged. "Forgot our ancestors were a bit shorter back then."

"Leave that open behind us," Joseph ordered. "We may need to make a fast escape, and if those dwarven reinforcements ever show up, hopefully they'll see and follow us." Stitch picked up the scent again, and Joseph led the party onward as quickly as he could without leaving himself vulnerable to ambush.

They had been dashing through the twists and turns of the tunnels for several minutes when Dorav called out, "I know where we are, now. And I'd bet glow fish to gold bars that I know where they're headed. They're going to the Well."

"What's that?" Joseph asked, still running.

"A shaft running straight down into the bedrock," Dorav answered. "Legends said it was bottomless. We've since learned that's impossible, of course, but we've never successfully sounded out its depth. If what you all call magic is what we all call the strange and unexplained, then that's probably the place."

"We've got Rook's scent. We'll find out when we get there."

"Right, it's only..."

"What?" Joseph growled.

"Well," Dorav hesitated. "If I'm right, I know a shortcut."

"Are you sure?" Kaillë asked.

"I'm sure about the shortcut. A rover never forgets a tunnel. But I can't be completely sure that's where they're going."

Joseph kept moving as he weighed his options. Dorav was right that a nearly-bottomless pit was probably the closest thing to a nearby place of magic, but Joseph only knew a little more about such things than Dorav. Stitch's nose was a sure thing, but the shortcut would save precious time if the destination was correct, and Joseph was desperate for every second. "This shortcut," he asked, "is the entrance behind us or ahead? It can't be worth it to backtrack."

"No," Dorav answered, "we'll be there in a minute or

two, right around the next bend."

"Alright, we'll risk it," Joseph answered. "If we can come in by a different entrance, we may be able to get the drop on the enemy, too, and we need every advantage we can get."

Just around the next bend, Dorav located a door in the right-hand wall that led into a narrow tunnel full of stale air. They kept a rapid pace for another quarter-hour, then Dorav stopped them at a blank stone wall. "The Well is just on the other side of this door," he murmured. "What do we do now, Joseph?"

"Dwarf doors are quiet," Joseph answered, "but someone is bound to see it open, so we won't have much time. Kaillë, stay out of sight unless you spot Rook and think you can free her. Elves, ready bows and take out as many targets as you can from the cover of the doorway. With any luck, any archers they have will be covering the other door, so drop them before they can adjust their focus. Waste no arrows on the Baron; if he's vulnerable, I will deal with him, and if not, your shots would do no good. Stitch," Joseph said to the dog leaning against his leg, "go lay down; you've done your part. Dorav, you're with me. Somehow we have to cut our way to the Baron and separate him from those stones. Everybody clear?"

Everyone nodded.

"Dorav...open the door."

Dorav pressed the wall, and the door sprang open.

~ * ~

The Well was perfectly round, as was the chamber that contained it, a thirty-foot ledge of stone running all the way around the fifty-foot-wide pit. Sentries were stationed around the room, but the majority were to the left, facing the main entrance to the cavern. Directly across from that, to Joseph's right, stood the Baron at the very edge of the pit, lit from below by a hellish flicker reaching up from the Well. A few feet behind him, Rook was bound and gagged, struggling against her bonds. The Baron held a glowing orb in his hand, and a pack slung over his shoulder surely contained the remaining eleven stones. He stood chanting and waving his arms; it appeared he had begun the ritual, but not yet reached its climax and the single moment of weakness that would present itself.

The elves' eyes were as quick as they were keen, and only a second after the door opened, half the Baron's archers were dead. Joseph had no concern the other half would live long enough to cause him a problem. Dorav charged out ahead of him and struck the nearest sentry like a thunderbolt, but not before he could raise the alarm. Half a dozen men stood between him and the Baron, and now the balance of the enemy were turning toward their comrade's shout. "Intruders!" shouted a familiar voice. It was Gren, rallying the main body of guards to turn from the door and counterattack.

Joseph caught a flash of movement to his right, but it made little impression as he picked up a sword from the guard Dorav had killed and advanced on the nearest enemy, holding the blade out to parry in his left hand and keeping his knife back in his right, poised to strike. Dorav stuck to his left flank for a moment, then turned to face the crowd now charging hard from behind. The guard thrust a spear at Joseph; he batted the point aside and hooked his sword behind the weapon's crossbar, slowing the enemy in drawing the weapon back and allowing Joseph to dance inside his reach and finish him off with the knife. A second guard wasn't ready for the sudden reversal of fortune as Joseph flipped and braced the fallen spear, and the man ran himself onto the point, his eyes wide with shock and pain. The other guards were a bit farther away, and Joseph hazarded a glance over his shoulder. Dorav was holding his own against the first wave of the Baron's men, thanks in large part to the elves slaying targets of opportunity as Dorav kept their attention. Still, five more men were about to join the fray, and Joseph saw others charging the door where the elves were sheltering. He looked back at the Baron, and his blood froze in his veins.

Baron Turov had paused his ritual and turned toward the skirmish. At that instant, though, he wasn't looking at Joseph or Dorav. His eyes were on Kaillë, who was kneeling next to Rook, cutting her free from her bonds. The Baron's lip curled in a vicious sneer as he started to raise his hand. Dorav shouted as he was brought down under the weight of too many attackers. The guards raced toward Joseph, their boots hammering the floor just as Joseph's heart hammered at his ribcage. The Baron began to thrust the orb at Rook and Kaillë.

Joseph dropped his knife as he let his bow slide from his shoulder and drew from his quiver the one arrow he had, knowing it would be useless against Turov. Ignoring the guards now just paces away, Joseph drew his bow, took aim, and loosed. The arrow flew fast and true, clanging against the glowing orb in Turov's hand. The sphere tumbled from his grasp, falling down into the unnatural depths of the Well. Crying out, the Baron reached for the stone, leaning out into space. The pack slid off his shoulder as he stretched, and its weight threw off his balance as it swung from the crook of his elbow. He threw his left arm back, trying desperately to keep his footing, but it was too late. His left foot came off the ground, he teetered crazily for a heartbeat, then he plunged down into the depths, carrying the Hoard into the fires below. At the last moment, Rook screamed and lunged forward, but Kaillë caught her arm and kept her from risking her own life as the magic of Dalviir slipped from her grasp.

The Hoard was gone. The Baron was dead. The world was safe.

Joseph was not.

The two nearest guards slammed into the hunter, and he shoved to the left as they struck, slicing his hand as he diverted a blade thrust from his heart into his shoulder. Growling at the pain, he delivered a compact uppercut to the first guard, sending him reeling back as he took the weapon from his foe and tore it free from his own flesh. Joseph skewered the second guard before he could react, knowing his wounds would soon render him useless in this battle. Two more guards were headed in his direction, but Rook and Kaillë were now on their feet and striking from behind, granting the larger men little chance. Joseph turned and hesitated for a moment, knowing the elves needed him and unsure whether it was too late to do anything for Dorav. Either way, his left arm was going cold and his right hand was slippery with blood. He was not to have a chance to decide. A figure broke free from the mob and loomed before him: Gren, armed with a broadsword and encased in steel armor.

"You have caused nothing but trouble, hunter," the guard captain sneered. "You're much more spry without a girl in your arms or a whip around your neck. I should have killed you myself when I had the chance instead of leaving it to those fools of Aglar's."

Joseph realized his shoulder wound must be bleeding faster than he'd thought as a wave of dizziness buffeted his skull. He gripped his knife hard, despite the blood, but his left-handed grip on the sword was weakening. He blinked hard and wracked his brain for a way to create an opening. "Are you gonna kill me," Joseph started, slurring his words, "or just keep talkin' 'til I jump down after your boss." He stumbled forward a few steps.

Gren took the bait. He laughed and swung his sword.

Joseph dropped and rolled, coming up on his knees at Gren's feet, and thrust his knife up into the warrior's unarmored groin. Gren screamed in pain and swung his sword's pommel down at Joseph's head, but before the strike could connect, Joseph scissored his legs, taking Gren's out from under him. Joseph's knife flashed in the firelight as he buried it under Gren's chin, silencing him for good.

Suddenly a chorus of growls resounded through the chamber, and a pack of badgers charged in through the main entrance as two hret-dialt units sprang from the side door Joseph's party had used. Joseph rolled onto his back as Rook and Kaillë ran up beside him. Rook stood looking down at him with flames in her eyes, but Kaillë wasted no time in seeing to his wounds with strips cut from a guard's uniform.

The well trained and perfectly coordinated hret-dialts of the dwarven guard made quick work of the Baron's leaderless mercenaries as Joseph allowed exhaustion to overtake him. The last thing he remembered was strong hands lifting him up onto a cart.

Chapter Thirteen

Joseph opened his eyes to the low, constant light of the dwarven city, knowing no way to guess the length of time he might have been unconscious. A powerful hunger clawed at his belly, and his left arm ached.

"Joseph?" a light voice asked from his right. "Joseph, are you awake?"

"Yeah," he croaked. "Where am I?"

"An infirmary back in the elders' tower," Kaillë explained, drawing close to Joseph's bedside. "They've taken very good care of you; you've been asleep for a whole day since the battle."

"I've been a little behind on rest," he said, "playing manservant to a bunch of runaway elves."

"Apologies. Shall I have someone get you something to eat?"

"Soon. First, how did everyone fare?" he asked.

"Rook was unhurt except a few bruises and injured pride. She was going to break into the vault, as we guessed, and had already sneaked past the first checkpoint when she heard the battle behind her. She ran forward to warn the rest of the guards, but when the Baron managed to fight his way to the vault, he forced her to open it to him. Losing the Hoard was quite a blow, too, but she's getting back on her feet, which, sadly, is more than we can say for her brother.

"You can see Dorav for yourself," Kaillë continued, pointing to a bed on the left. Joseph looked over to see the dwarf lying there, heavily bandaged and still. "He took many wounds, but he is strong. I believe he will get better in time. Steva is on the mend as well." Joseph heard a grunt and craned his neck to see the huge badger curled up at the foot of Dorav's bed. Stitch dozed on the great badger's back, forcing Joseph to chuckle, which sent mild shocks of pain through his shoulder, and only then did he realize his left arm was bound in a sling.

"Ten'daren, Ten'vahlë, and Ten'sael are unhurt..." Kaillë continued, "...but Tes'oriv did not survive his wounds. When the Baron's men charged their hiding place, Tes'oriv held until the last, emptying his quiver just as the enemy reached him. He held them back as long as he could after that. The others are alive now because of him. He did his duty. Tal'onë will be proud of him."

"I'm sorry," Joseph said.

"He was not," Kaillë answered. "At the end, he said, 'Tell Azrith it was an honor to serve him, by any name.'"

"He will not be forgotten," Joseph replied after a time. He looked back at Dorav then, hoping the dwarf would stir, and Kaillë left to request food.

~ * ~

Joseph would have preferred to let his group rest for a few days before heading back, or for that matter to wait until his left arm was mobile, but he knew Kaillë's people would be awaiting her return, so the next day they prepared to set out. The dwarves seemed more affronted by the offense of being robbed than the loss of the stones themselves in what they chose to call a 'recovery effort'. With Dorav still not lucid, the dwarves had no way to guess it was Rook who'd actually broken into the vault, and Joseph was not inclined to help them make that connection. He was confident Dorav would stay silent about it when, and if, he recovered.

Indeed, the dwarves had no idea Joseph and the elves had saved their entire clan from annihilation, and they considered his volunteering to fight alongside them only a strange surface-walker custom, if an appreciated one. No, the thing the dwarves valued was a chance to learn more about the poultices Joseph and Kaillë had used, for the loss of too many faithful badgers had evidently been a plague on the dwarven military for generations. The elders sent the surface-walkers on their way under the condition they would return to the Ninth Clan's domain, by a more direct route, with a store of medicinal herbs, prepared to negotiate a treaty of trade between the clans to begin a stable supply. Kaillë, not a profit-taker by nature, offered simply to teach the dwarves what to look for so that they could harvest their own, but the elders shunned that idea, explaining that while they claimed absolute possession of all things under the earth, they claimed no right to anything under the sky and would not consider taking any plants directly.

Dwarven guards escorted their new allies to a busier tunnel that led to a portal not unlike the one Joseph had stumbled into during the war, a cave below the tree line that cut a day out of their return travel. They bore Tes'oriv's remains with them, wrapped in a dwarven funereal shroud. "If you want to lay him to rest in your village," Joseph said, "it's only a couple hours out of the way from here."

"That is not our custom," Kaillë said. "We will leave his mortal flesh to the elements and creatures of the wood, that they may take his body for nourishment as we take theirs."

The day was just dawning, and a chill had settled over the land while they were underground. Frost covered the fallen leaves of the forest floor as the band found a tranquil spot to lay Tes'oriv. With deep reverence, Ten'daren and Ten'vahlë removed the burial robe as Ten'sael presented the bundle of Tes'oriv's pack, weapons, and clothing to Kaillë, saying in Elven, "As Tes'oriv had no heir, we offer his possessions to the greatest good of the clan."

Kaillë received the bundle, then prayed, "As Oriv came into this world, so Tes'oriv leaves it, unburdened by the trappings of life and surrounded by those who love him. We will sing his song and wait for him to greet us in the next world."

The elves turned away then, leaving Tes'oriv to be reclaimed by the woods.

"Rook," Kaillë said after they had walked for a time, "I'm sorry for what happened. I know our way of life must seem very crude to someone used to the bustle of the city, but you can stay with the Windriders as long as you like."

"Nah," Rook answered, adjusting her pack on her shoulders. "Dalviir's Hoard isn't the only wonder left in the world. Something out there will heal my brother, and I'm going to find it. Tall, dark, and wounded over here is no good to me now, anyway. I'm heading my own way, and I suppose now is as good a time as any. Track me down when you get out of that sling, hunter. I've got some ideas on how you can pay me back for those stones you owe me." She winked at Kaillë and slipped off into the woods, leaving no trace she'd been there.

They walked on, and Joseph knitted his brows and scowled. "What is it, Joseph?" Kaillë asked when she noticed his expression.

"I'm...uneasy," he replied.

"Again?" What is it this time?"

"Aglar and the Baron never would have made it to the

vault if the guard hadn't been distracted by the troll attack. What were the odds of the trolls going at the main gate at just the right moment?"

"You think the trolls were working for the Baron somehow?" Kaillë asked, incredulous.

"No, that's impossible. The Baron didn't even know the Hoard was going to be there ahead of time, and there's no way he could have coordinated something like that on the run."

"So, you said it yourself, it's impossible. There is such a thing as a coincidence, Joseph."

"You're probably right," he agreed, but the scowl didn't leave his face.

"So, Joseph," Kaillë said after a few moments, "you've done more than your duty, and the danger has passed. Your forest is safe again. What will you do now?"

Joseph looked off to the southwest. When he'd left his camp to go hunting a week before, it had never crossed his mind he might not return. He'd left a number of things there, but nothing he couldn't replace. The only thing holding him was Delia's grave, but he knew whatever she might have wanted for him after her death, it wouldn't have had anything to do with some old bones she had shed years ago. At last he looked back at Kaillë. "First," he said, "I'm going to get you home."

"Home?" Kaillë rebutted. "I don't know where that is anymore, Joseph."

"Well, then..." he said, "...then I guess it might take quite a while."

Kaillë smiled up at him, then turned and led the scouts to the south, toward her people. And Joseph, the Spirit of the Trees, went with them.

Epilogue

The flames in the Well had finally gone cold, plunging the chamber into perfect darkness, a darkness so complete it seemed any light would be swallowed up by it rather than dispelling it. There was something in that darkness, something that should never be, and for the first time in many long ages of dwarves, elves, and men, that something spoke, and its voice was as hard as the stones and as cold as the void, as bitter and inevitable as the grave.

"Rise, Baron. Bringing me the stones does not end your service to me. Not even death can do that. Rise, Baron. Your work is only beginning."

About the Author

Shane L. Coffey lives in Colorado with his wife and the multitude of characters trying to fight their way from his brain to his computer screen. He is a man of simple tastes, inexpensive hobbies, and little travel...but if anybody starts making plans for an expedition to Mars or Rivendell, he'll be very interested to know whether they require any skillsets he possesses (...or could convincingly fake).

Turn the page for a preview of Volume III: Calamity...

CALAMITY
The Spirit of the Trees: Volume III

Chapter Six: Abomination

Preparations for the mission were made in haste, but sussing out the destination took some time. The Windriders kept no maps, and Dorav was unfamiliar with the surface. Still, after repeated description of the location of the first troll attacks and much scratching in the dirt and with charcoal sticks on bark scraps, all while Dorav checked and rechecked his subterranean charts, the band managed to merge their collective knowledge to determine the tunnel the trolls must have used. It was mid-morning by the time they were ready to set out, and the rising sun was warming the forest...a bit too quickly for Joseph's taste.

"If we don't return," he told Kaillë, "you need to pack up your clan and get out of here while you can."

"Don't say that," Kaillë argued, her eyes bright with tears that didn't flow. "You have to come back."

It was with a deep ache that Joseph separated from Kaillë's embrace and turned toward the trees, passing Tal'onë as he did. He glanced over his shoulder to ensure Kaillë was out of earshot before speaking in low tones to the captain. "If the worst does happen," he said, "see she gets to safety. Promise me that."

Tal'onë nodded then Joseph left him behind as well and

moved to where Tes'sael was marshalling the picked force that would accompany Joseph and Dorav to the tunnel mouth.

"Are you certain you're rested enough for this?" Joseph asked Tes'sael.

"I'll have to be," the elf replied. "Tal'onë and Tes'voran will be too sorely needed here if we fail. Besides, I've slept long enough. Are you ready to move out, Joseph?"

Joseph looked to Dorav, and the dwarf grunted his assent. Tes'sael made a motion to two owl-riders that sent them scouting aloft in a downdraft of buffeting wings, then the band set off into the trees.

With Dorav along, the going was slower than Joseph would have liked, but he needed the dwarf's knowledge of stonecraft to block the tunnel, especially as the Windriders were painfully light on tools. The hunter brought the dogs along as well to alert the band to any strange scents, and Stitch barely left Dorav's side. The dwarf often complained about the dog being too close and getting in his way, but Joseph noticed the old rover dropping his hand to scratch behind Stitch's ears when he thought nobody was looking.

It was midday when the band reached the tunnel mouth. The owl riders had reported nothing unusual, but Joseph was cautious as he led his company on their final approach. He sent the riders to trees farther up the slope to keep watch and fly back to the village with warning if anything should go wrong. Dorav he kept in the cover of a thicket with Tes'sael and another elf guarding him, his ability to work the stone making him the only indispensable member of their mission. Joseph crept forward with the six remaining elves, peering into the shadows of the tunnel; Yowler was next to him, sniffing the air and ground but not showing any alarm. Joseph spotted some scat that matched no natural creatures of his forest, giving him confidence the trolls indeed had come this way, but by Yowler's lack of reaction, he hoped they had retreated as the cold descended and were nowhere near. Still, the day grew warmer, and he resisted the urge to doff his cloak as much for wishful thinking as anything else.

At last they reached the shadows under the tunnel, and Joseph motioned for the elf to his right to light a torch. The orange glow drove back the darkness, and Joseph saw a few fresh bones gnawed too clean even to stink, but otherwise the tunnel was deserted. A motion to another elf sent the scout hustling noiselessly back to the trees, bringing Dorav and the rest of the band to their side a moment later. The dwarf spoke no words before setting to his work, placing an ear against the stone wall before tapping it with a hammer, then creasing his forehead in thought before moving to another spot and repeating the process. This was interspersed with running back and forth from the tunnel to the overhead slope with a string that was knotted at regular intervals and wrapped around a stone cylinder, about the size of a hand drum, with a spiral groove and dwarven characters marking each turn. Before the first trip he motioned the closest elf over to the spot where he was standing and pressed the free end of the string into the elf's hand with an order to "hold the dumb end." On future trips he would just point to an elf with the measuring device and expect to be understood. Finally, after marking several locations on the slope overhead with his chisel, Dorav ordered some of the elves to boost him up to the tunnel roof, which took more of them than he seemed to think right, then repeated his hammer soundings on the ceiling. Satisfied, he returned to the outside slope, measured an offset from each of his prior marks, and marked the new location.

"Alright," he said, pulling a long, steel gouge from the side of his pack, "who's got a decent mallet?"

One of the elves stepped forward with a large, wooden hammer.

"Give that to Joseph," the dwarf grunted. "You're too

damn small."

"They're stronger than they look," Joseph assured the dwarf.

"Stronger than you?"

"...No."

"Then get over there and start pounding. I need a channel running from the mark on that far end to the one over here, passing through each of the ones in between. That's the new marks, mind, the old ones were just for setup."

"How deep?" Joseph asked.

"'Bout a hand-span. The rest of you lot, find some good clay soil and start making piles next to the trench. Understand?"

Tes'sael translated for about half the band whose human speech was still rudimentary, then they all set to their work, Dorav using hammer and chisel to start at the nearer mark with the intention of meeting Joseph in the middle.

The going was slow for Joseph, but Dorav's arms and tools chewed through the stone like a hungry wolf chewing through tallow. He met up with Joseph's trench only a quarter of the way from Joseph's end, finishing triple the work of the human in the hour they had both spent. Joseph wiped his brow, his cloak long since discarded, and shook his head in amazement at the dwarf's speed. "I suspected you were stronger than I," Joseph said, catching his breath, "but I hadn't thought so much stronger."

Dorav eyed the sides of Joseph's narrow trench. "I'm not sure it's a matter of strength. I've been working with stone my whole life, after all, and...well, you seem to be working *against* it."

Joseph was expert enough in his own craft to understand precisely what Dorav meant, but as for applying it to the unyielding stone he'd been sweating over for the last hour, he had no idea.

Dorav paced over to his pack, a few feet from the far

end of the new channel, and put away his tools then removed a coil of rope, or at least something that looked rope-like. Unraveling the coil, the dwarf counted off a number of turns that looked to Joseph to about match the length of their trench. As he looked more closely, the hunter realized what he had first taken for rope was actually a fine mesh of something like wool, with crabapple-sized bulges every hand-span or so down its length.

"What's that?" Joseph asked.

"Blast rope," Dorav answered. "Each bulb is a little charge, all with staggered fuses so you just light one end of the rope and they all blow at once. 'Course, the longer you're into the coil, the faster you get the 'Boom', so you don't want to lose track of how much you've used. But they're made to a standard length, so it's pretty easy to tell."

Joseph had seen firsthand the dwarves' advanced knowledge of crafts and strictly-structured society during his sojourn there the previous autumn, so nothing Dorav said surprised him, but seeing such precision in action again, he couldn't help but admire it. Living in that kind of culture would have smothered Joseph nearly to death, but he respected it for its own merits.

Starting at his end of the trench with the freshest-cut end of his blast rope, Dorav laid the explosive into the newly dug seam of stone. Once he was a few feet down, he motioned for the surrounding elves to start filling the trench with the clay soil they'd prepared. "Pack that down good, now," he instructed. "The better the pack, the more force will—"

Yowler, standing nearby, was pawing at the ground, and Stitch, nearer the cave mouth, let loose a throaty, growling bark.

"Stay here!" Joseph ordered the detail he had left to guard Dorav before approaching the cave. He motioned for the rest to follow, unslinging his bow, which he'd kept strung all day.

Joseph and the elves bounded down the slope to the tunnel mouth, peering into the dark. The sun was only a little past its zenith, lighting but a few feet into the westward-facing cave. Joseph saw that the elf to his left was lighting a torch, and as soon as it was burning well he took it and heaved it into the darkness. The elves gasped and cursed at what it revealed.

Seething from the deeper reaches of the caverns were half a dozen trolls scrabbling abreast up the tunnel, and behind them half a dozen more, and a like number beyond that, farther back than the torch could show. Their black fur seemed to catch and hoard the meager light, bringing the darkness with them from the depths; their bat-like noses and ears flared in recognition of nearby food.

"Eyes and throats!" Joseph ordered in Elven as he stretched his bow. A handful of arrows hissed out on either side of Joseph, and trolls fell screaming to be trampled by the ranks behind.

"Blow the tunnel, Dorav!" Joseph shouted up the slope. "Blow it now!"

If the dwarf replied, Joseph did not hear it as he loosed arrows at the trolls in lightning succession. The elves Joseph had selected were the best in the camp; one or two even rivaled his own skill with the bow. Trolls fell in waves, arrows sticking out from their faces, but there always seemed to be more to replace them, and Joseph's quiver was getting light.

Still, Joseph noticed the onslaught was slowing. With each rank of dead trolls to climb over, the rest seemed more reluctant to charge forward; it was the only hint of reason Joseph had ever seen in them. In another few moments the mob had halted altogether, milling about as if waiting. The archers, eager to conserve what arrows they could, stopped their counter-attack.

"Half a minute more, Joseph," the hunter heard Tes'sael shout in the Elven tongue. Joseph eyed the rippling trollish mob and gritted his teeth.

"On my mark," Joseph growled, pulling a shaft from his quiver and nocking it to his bowstring. He had only four or five arrows more. He raised his bow and took aim. "Stretch!"

The line of archers pulled their bows, loosing at the end of their reach. At this less frenetic pace, every arrow found its mark, and seven trolls fell dead. The horde pulled back a little. Joseph gave the order to repeat the salvo, but even as arrows were drawn, a path opened in the crowd of trolls and a tall figure strode into the torchlight. Ragged, purple robes hung from his frame; the hair was missing from the right half of his head, replaced with a shiny burn scar, and a black eyepatch hid his right eye. His lips were pulled back in a wolfish grin as his one-eyed gaze pinned Joseph.

Joseph's jaw hung agape, for the thing standing before him could not be. The man he saw was dead, killed, more or less, by Joseph's own hand. Yet the eye, the grin, the robes were all unmistakable: Baron Turov, murderer of the Windrider elves, thief of the Hoard of Dalviir, and sent by Joseph to his inevitable death at the fiery bottom of the dwarven Well more than six months ago.

Turov, if indeed the thing was him, reached to his face and tore off the eyepatch, revealing an empty socket underneath, the blackness of its depths seeming to reach back forever, broken only by a single point of bilious, pallid light in its center. Revealing that light seemed to dispel some sort of glamor that masked the baron's true face to reveal a grinning death's head, cracked and charred as by intense heat. The wan twinkle flared into a hideous green flame, and suddenly the bow fell from Joseph's hand as his arms went numb. He gasped for breath, but his ribs were being squeezed as by cords of steel, letting no air in. The sensation of constriction inched upward to his throat; the hunter scrabbled meekly at his neck with enfeebled arms, but there was nothing tangible to pull away. Seeing his distress, elves launched arrows with renewed vigor, but those striking the Baron seemed to do no harm, drawing only a hideous cackle from his immolated face, and the trolls surged forward once more.

All the elves dropped their bows and drew long knives or axes; the four nearest Joseph stepped forward to protect him as he dropped to his knees, his lungs burning, while the other two leapt forward, hurling themselves into the seething, black horde. Joseph tried to scream for them to stop, but he could no more force his voice out than he could draw air in.

Suddenly a low *whumpf* sounded from the stone overhead, and a shower of small rocks and dust rained down on the melee, not heavy enough to obscure the sight of one of the elves being slashed across the face with ragged claws while another, his arms pinned by two trolls, had his throat ripped out by the razor maw of a third. Barely a moment later, a series of piercing cracks sounded from the stone, followed by a shake and rumble as the whole hillside slid down on the cavern, burying troll and elf and revenant alike. The last thing Joseph saw before a massive stone slab blocked the cave mouth was the sickly flame of the Baron's eye, and even after Joseph's breath returned in a *whoosh* and silence settled over the forest, he could still hear that awful cackling in his mind. Whatever vile craft preserved the Baron from the hellish flames of the deepest earth, Joseph knew a few tons of rock would give it no pause. The contradiction was impossible to reconcile, but he couldn't deny the facts: Baron Turov was surely dead, and just as surely walked the earth once more.

Calamity is available at www.burnthemap.com

I9781949700015
FICTION COF
Coffey, Shane L.,
Identity and Community :

EARLVILLE FREE LIBRARY
4 N. Main Street
Earlville, NY 13332
(315) 691-5931

CPSIA information can
at www.ICGtesting.com
Printed in the USA
LVHW041539080819
626994LV000